ALEX LIDELL

LAST CHANCE
REFORM

IMMORTALS OF TALONSWOOD

SCOUT

TRACING SHADOWS (Audiobook available)

UNRAVELING DARKNESS (Audiobook available)

TILDOR

THE CADET OF TILDOR

SIGN UP FOR NEW RELEASE NOTIFICATIONS at https://links.alexlidell.com/News

---

Reese

*R*eese pulled off the second set of bloodied latex gloves and disposed of them before pulling on new ones. Once, the smell of so much fae blood would have made his stomach growl in hunger. Now it just made it churn. Or maybe it was this particular scent.

Standing over Ellis, whose whipped back resembled something out of a meat grinder, Reese contemplated his treatment plan. Asher had gone as light as he dared in laying the lashes and stayed clear of the kidneys, but that concentrated the punishment over Ellis's shoulders. A hundred lashes did damage no matter how little enthusiasm with which they were laid.

Which Count Victor had known full well when he'd ordered it. Quinn might have been a sadistic bastard, but he was also Victor's coddled protégé, so his death could not have gone unpunished.

"Admiring the view?" Ellis turning his head toward Reese.

The male's face was pale for a warmblood, his hand curled in a white-knuckle grip around the edge of the table. But his voice was steady. Conversational. Ellis was too well trained and too thoroughly damaged to allow pain to leak into his words if he wanted to keep it under wraps.

"The whip was iron tipped. It's not going to let your magic heal it quickly, and there is only so much I can do to flush out the iron."

"Tell me something I don't know, Doc."

Reese let the title go. Over the last few centuries, he'd been anything the special forces had a need for. Demolitions. Recon. Black ops. Medic. Ellis was still searching for whatever title would get under Reese's skin the most, and *doc* was the current favorite. It was an especially effective jab because placing Reese in the infirmary had been one of Count Victor's changes since he took over running Talonswood a week ago.

The other amusing novelties had included installing a high-tech lock system that kept the cadets to their rooms, stripping Asher of most of his power as the Academy's commander, and, of course, demonstrating his new no-one-is-above-the-rules-especially-fae routine by having Ellis flogged before the whole school.

Ten cadets had passed out by the end of that little demonstration, and another dozen lost their breakfast.

Appearances aside, Victor was Asher's opposite when it came to running things. Not altogether surprising since Victor enjoyed presiding over a court while Asher came into his own through commanding armies. Thus, spitting in the face of Asher's strict military discipline, Victor promptly canceled morning exercises, allowed students off campus during liberty days, played favorites to whoever bowed the lowest, and generally turned a selective blind eye to speciesism between the different creatures. Under Victor's new regime, the cadets were regressing to impulsivity alarmingly fast.

"Didn't the witch pull out some iron from the manacles when you were in the cage?" Reese asked, trying to fit the injured flesh together. It was like a bloody mosaic.

"Do not even start." Ellis's voice hardened, the note of murderous steel in it undiminished by the fact that he was lying on Reese's medical table, utterly vulnerable to anything the vamp might do. In truth, Reese didn't know how the warmblood could stand it. "Samantha stays out of this."

"You'd heal faster with her help," Reese pointed out, though it was an effort to keep his voice even. He himself would never accept a witch's aid, but professionalism pushed him to offer his patient the option. Ellis was badly off, no matter how much the warrior pretended otherwise.

"The witch is my mate," Ellis snapped, now swinging himself into a sitting position, yellow eyes flashing. His pale blond hair hung in sweaty strands around his blanched face. "And you are not telling her that something that will cause her agony is a good idea."

Oh, they were onto *that*.

"Then how about I tell you to get the hell out of Talonswood?" Reese snapped. "It would do all of us a favor. What the hell is keeping you here now? Fear of Daddy?"

"You know exactly what's keeping me," Ellis snarled, his rolling Highlands accent thick with fury. "And if you haven't worked it out already, Samantha Devinee is very likely not just my mate, but yours too. And Asher's and Cassis's. It's been near four hundred years since the four of us were in the same place. Do you think all this is an accident?"

"I don't take mates," Reese said, his hands opening and closing at his sides. He didn't take mates. He didn't so much as take women for more than a night, and usually only if he paid for their services. He'd learned the hard way what giving a piece of your soul to a woman could do. Cassis's lover, a powerful witch named Sienna, had hurt them all during those ten years she'd kept them captive—but the worst had come when she'd discovered just how much physical abuse Reese could endure and changed tactics. When she'd dragged his wife into the lair and butchered her before Reese's eyes while he beat himself against the magic restraining him, something inside him had slammed shut. No woman—no one—was worth that risk. That pain. Asher, who'd also lost a lover to Sienna's machinations might understand, but Reese doubted Ellis ever could.

Reese shook his head, snapping himself back to the present. Four hundred years ago, the screams of Reese's wife had destroyed him. But that was the past. He was stronger now, the scar tissue over his soul keeping out all the things that could hurt him. That was what made him deadly. And efficient. And it was the reason he was not going to play Ellis's game.

"Does Sam even know any of your brilliant theory?" Reese asked. "Does *she* think she's mated to you?"

"Of course not." Ellis's eyes narrowed. "I'm certain the connection is due to Sienna's work, and Sam deserves better than that. Her own life. Her own choices."

"Hades, have you spoken to her at all since the deed? You bedded the witch, Ellis. In my experience, females require some conversation after the fact."

"No. And I don't plan to. Bedding Devinee was a mistake I don't intend to repeat. She's better off without me. Which you very well know."

"So now you're just going to… What? Lurk in the shadows and protect her from threats unknown?" There was nothing kind in Reese's voice. He meant the words to hurt. Putting his hands on the edge of the treatment table where the male sat, Reese loomed over him. "For the record, this sounds exactly like the kind of self-flagellation you're fond of, Ellis. You'll forgive me if I don't applaud your damn masochism. And I am certainly not jumping into your sinking boat."

"Why *are* you here, Reese?" Ellis asked, turning the tables with one lifted eyebrow and keeping a better grip on his temper than Reese would have given the male credit for. "At Talonswood."

Reese chuckled without humor. "Because I'm dead." He needed to lie low for a few years while the humans forgot about his latest identity, this time an American SEAL killed in Afghanistan—the hazard of being an immortal in the mortal world. Faking your own death and starting anew every few years. Sometimes in the same country, but most often not. But maybe Ellis had a point. Three years was long enough. It was time to leave. Reese picked up a clear vial. "Lie the hell back down so I can be done unfucking this mess—though you are going to be useless for a week or two no matter what I do. With iron in your blood, I can't even make analgesics work. It's down to salves and antibiotics."

"I don't need antibiotics to fight off this world's germs. I'm hardly a cub." The glower Ellis gave to the syringe Reese started filling made him snort. For someone who could face a terrifying flogging without any outward fear, Ellis's dislike of needles was an absurdity Reese could not begin to unravel.

"Then stop acting like one. Settle down and look the fuck away." Reese held up the syringe right in front of Ellis's face, letting the bead of medicine squirt from the needle. "Or better yet, watch me closely. I enjoy seeing you blanch."

2

Sam

Quinn shoves me over the edge of the bed, his hands cruel. Powerful. His hand clamps over my neck, his rough tongue licking my terror-filled sweat. I fight. I try to fight. But I can't. Not against a vampire twice my size. The helplessness rakes through me, ripping my soul until I scream.

My scream merges with another's. Cassis lies strapped to a worktable, roaring in pain as a witch named Sienna carves into his flesh. I struggle to move, to get to him. But I can't. Helplessness cuts through me again. I try to bite back my hollers of pain, as if silence can end this.

My silence stays as the scene changes again. The crack of an iron-tipped whip against flesh the only sound to be heard in the Academy training yard, Ellis's blood soaking his pants and dripping onto the cold earth. No, don't!—I open my mouth to shout to Asher, but no sound comes out. Ellis sags silently against the whipping post. Asher brings back his arm. I can't stop it.

I sit bolt upright, hitting my knees against the bottom of my writing desk, the snippets of nightmare lingering in the quiet dorm room. My open notebook, where I was writing an essay on the history of the fae-vampire wars, is blotched with sweat stains.

Damn.

I'm getting no sleep at night, so I'm not surprised that the fae-vampire wars knocked me right out. I rub my stinging knees and head to the suite's bathroom to shower, examining the liquid soap before daring to touch it. Two days ago, my neighbors—a pair of waifish demivamps who coincidentally grew up on the same posh street in London and purr about it at least once a day—found peroxide somewhere and poured it into my shampoo. The day before that, they managed to rub nettle extract on the toilet paper.

Bracing my head against the cool tile, I let the steamy water wash away the cold sweat and dregs of memory. Quinn is dead. So is Sienna. Ellis is alive and healing. At least I hope he is. Besides yesterday's punishment, I haven't seen him since he killed Quinn to save me. Killed Quinn so that I didn't have to—and didn't have to be the one with Asher's whip permanently marking my mortal skin. I can see the green again now, the blood sprouting from Ellis's skin with each blow.

Every day that passes without seeing him, the cage seems more and more like a dream—connecting our scars, drawing away his pain, feeling him move inside me. But I can't find a way to be allowed into the same room as him even for a few minutes, and it's not for lack of trying.

My lungs tighten painfully, struggling against the hot, steamy air. The morning after Quinn's attack, I went to Asher's office, begging the commander to let me into the guards' holding cell. He kicked me out. I went the next day and the next, and finally—probably worried he'd kill me himself out of sheer annoyance—Asher went to ask if Ellis could receive a visitor.

Asher's words still ring in my head, making my chest ache. *He doesn't want to see you.*

With a towel wrapped around me, I return to the room and glance at the clock. Only twenty minutes until lunch. Pulling my sketch journal from my desk, I give my pencil free rein to stroke the nightmares onto paper, as if that can help leave them here in the room. It's time to pull myself together. A clean blue uniform skirt. A pressed white shirt. The appearance of cold calm.

I might be able to do nothing about what Sienna did all those centuries ago, but I'm done being helpless. Done being a victim where others have to come save me and pay the price. The morbidly amusing thing is that, until Ellis, there had never been anyone *to* come help. And for one stupid moment, I thought the change was good.

Right up until I watched the male's blood color the grass on the green, his own brother wielding the whip that did it.

If that's the cost of protecting me, I'll do my own protecting, thank you very much. Like I always have—for both myself and my foster sister, Janie. I may be a million years from my old life, but Janie is still there, and she needs me to survive and get out of here. I just need to get with the new program. With the new rules.

Standing before the mirror, I pull my hair back into a ponytail and then change my mind and shake it loose, letting the rebellious red-dyed brown streaks catch the streams of sunlight. I am Samantha Devinee, and I survived the New Jersey foster system. I ran a damn good burglary gig. I am a witch capable of summoning a storm—by sheer accidental instinct, but still.

Taking a deep breath, I let my spine straighten and my

shoulders roll back until the girl looking back from the mirror matches what I need her to be. Fake it until you make it. And I will make it.

I will be strong. An army of one, without all the uniforms and orders. I will be a witch who bends a knee to no one. Who needs no one's help.

Giving my reflection a nod, I head for the door. The light above the newly installed lock blinks green—one of several changes that Victor's made as the new dean. As much as I hate being locked in at night like a juvie detainee, I can't say I miss nightly fire watch and morning physical training. The count, in his own words, takes a more modern approach to education, believing Asher's military strictures "uncivilized for the current day."

Not that *modern* and *Count Victor* are words that anyone with half a brain would ever think of using together, but I'm not going to complain. If it lets me leave this claustrophobic place on the weekends, I'm all for it.

Unfortunately, afternoon combat training is still alive and well, so I'll just need to find a way not to get my ass handed to me this afternoon.

Outside, the green is disgusting, the vast grass lawn and dirt training yard, soup soft after a morning of rain. A cold wind carrying the remaining light drizzle cuts into my skin.

Stepping tenderly on the squishy earth, I pick my way slowly across the green toward the dining hall. At least the attention to my footing gives me a good reminder to avoid making eye contact with anyone. Fae and vamps, even demis, are strange about that. I'm pretty sure that if given a chance, they'd be going around pissing on trees to mark their territory and baring their teeth at imagined challenges.

"Move along, butcher bitch." The shove comes from behind, but I'm familiar enough with Christian's tactics by now to hold my balance. His girlfriend, Leanne, laughs lightly, as if watching a show put on just for her.

Stepping aside, I let the perfectly coiffed demivamps pass in a cloud of cologne, saving the fight for another day. One where I don't end up wet, cold, and muddy for the satisfaction of getting my nose broken. Even with my face lowered, I can see the smug smile on Christian's beautiful olive-skinned face.

"Fuck it, Christian. Don't send that shit here," a rough voice says. Hands on hips, a pack of four demifae cadets block the path I was going to take around Christian and his crowd. Snarling at me, the demifae pack leader, an older cadet with dark sideburns and hair as messy as Wolverine's, bares elongated canines. He has pale yellow eyes like Ellis, but his have a greenish glint, like stomach bile. Glaring at the splashes of mud my sidestep left on his boot, Wolverine shoves me back toward Christian.

"Butcher bitch is a warmblood," Leanne protests. "If you can't keep track of your trash, Wayne—"

Right.

"You know what? Fuck you both," I tell the two mini-gang leaders, Christian and Wayne the Wolverine, my voice the epitome of politeness. "I'm going to go eat. But please, don't stop your pissing war on my account."

Setting my sights on the dining hall door, I take a determined step forward.

Wayne's hairy arm wraps around my waist, yanking me off my feet and shoving me right into the vamps.

Fuck.

I land against Christian's chest, forcing him to take a step for balance. He nearly slips in the muddy grass and curses, shoving me back toward the demifae. I trip and land hard, hitting my head on the ground. The world shifts for a moment, a warm trickle of blood running down my temple. I quickly push up to my knees, wiping away the blood that has the demivamps smacking their lips. One thing working at Dusk has taught me is that free-flowing blood will always get attention. My heart pounds, my breath picking up speed as the demifae and demivamps square off against each other—with me in the middle. Trapped. Between two walls of testosterone and animal instinct.

"You dead-fuckers are the next extinct race," Wayne snarls, his skin rippling as if his muscles can't decide whether they're supposed to shift or not. Some demifae can, though most can't. I hope he's among the latter. Though, based on his raw-meat scent, I don't think I'll get that lucky. "Maybe you should take —*fuck!*" He cuts off as someone's fist cracks his nose, blood spraying onto his white uniform shirt.

The demivamps growl, probably salivating at the smell.

Taking advantage of the commotion, I shove my way backward toward elusive safety, never taking my eyes off the brawl. The demis hit hard and heal fast. I don't.

Wayne swipes his forearm across his face, his yellow eyes flashing at Christian. The demifae pulls back one massive hairy-knuckled fist, readying for a blow.

I inch myself farther from the middle, catching a shove from someone—Leanne, I think—to help me on my way. My foot slips. Wheeling backward through the mud, I brace myself for a cold, wet landing—and hit a hard wall of muscle instead.

"Enough," snaps a cold sophisticated voice, a strong hand gripping my elbow to keep me upright.

Everyone stops moving. Stops breathing.

Trailing my eyes up the long, manicured fingers at my elbow, I find Count Victor's cool dark eyes and swallow a curse. A step behind the new dean, Reese stands with his arms over his chest, his pale, beautiful face hard.

Unreadable. He wears his usual black fatigues and T-shirt, his dark messy hair the only thing on him that defies the perfect military order.

Victor lets go of my elbow and steps away to regard us all. Christian and the other demivamps drop to their knees before the count, the cold mud seeping through their uniforms. The demifae and I stand at attention. The air around us vibrates with tension, the attention of everyone on the green boring into our backs.

A bird sings from its hideout in a nearby maple, the only sound breaking the silence.

With long, deliberate strides, Victor walks along our line, his crisp black suit cutting an intimidating shape against the gray sky. Tall, dark-haired, and leanly muscled, he might be handsome if it weren't for the dead-fish pallor of his skin, the chilling ice in his gaze.

When he steps into a puddle that sends mud splashing all over Christian's face, the demi holds still, not flinching. Not daring to wipe his face. Hell, he probably considers Victor's boot mud sacred. As if cued by my thought, Leanna, who is the closest to where Victor has just stopped, leans down to kiss his boot, her thick black hair brushing the ground.

Victor ignores her, studying first the kneeling vamps, then the rest of us. The demifae stare straight ahead, military style, their faces blank. No respect for the count there, but plenty of fear. If Asher were here, we'd all be bear-crawling around the green for the next hour. But now, with Victor... There isn't a pattern to what he might do, with everything from light reprimand to an Ellis-style flogging on the table. Fear swirls sourly in my gut.

"Samantha." The vampire comes to a stop in front of me, his courteous voice holding an air of expectation. When I look up to meet his dark eyes, he raises a brow.

Clearing my throat, I offer the new dean a half bow. "Thank you for helping me keep my balance, sir," I say.

Behind him, Reese shifts his feet.

Victor smiles coolly, a hint of sharpened canines flashing behind his lips. "I am always glad to be of service, Samantha. However, the current situation seems slightly more complex, does it not?"

Apparently.

"You pushed me," Victor prompts.

The air on the green grows heavy, the kneeling demivamps somehow shrinking into themselves without moving a muscle. My heart starts to pound, my body seeming to know something before I do.

"I was pushed into you, sir," I answer, despite my churning stomach. There's not getting between two angry dogs, and then there's lying down in dog shit. I've never been good at the latter. "And I do thank you for preventing my fall. I'm certain I'd be in the mud otherwise right now."

Someone gasps to my left—it sounds like Christian, a fact I'd enjoy if the circumstances were any less...murdery feeling. Behind Victor, Reese wearily rubs his eyes with the heel of his hand. The count merely studies me with the curiosity of a child examining a bug beneath a magnifying glass. A heartbeat passes. "Are you expecting me to say *you are welcome*, perhaps?" A corner of Victor's mouth twitches up. "Or maybe *it was my pleasure?*"

I know the question is a trap, but apparently, I'm suicidal. And I'm out of better ideas. "Both good options, sir."

A muscle ticks in Victor's jaw, and for just a moment, I see the coldhearted thousand-year-old royal behind the dean's composed appearance. Like a glamour being lifted, Victor's dark eyes flash with cruel, powerful, Machiavellian truth. But just as quickly, it's gone, and his face is bland and only mildly interested once more. He turns to Reese. "Is this what Asher has been teaching cadets these past years?"

"The Academy has been following military protocol, not vampiric, Your Excellence," Reese replies evenly, his low, controlled voice holding all the lethal power of his body. When he turns his attention on me, my stomach tightens, his silent disapproval somehow more potent than a hundred of Victor's games. "That said, Devinee should have known better regardless."

"I see." Shifting his attention back to us, Victor turns toward Christian, speaking over his bent, trembling head. "The fae cannot control their base instincts, but I expected better of you. Have you anything to say?"

Christian touches his already mud-splattered forehead to the soggy ground. "Yes, Your Excellence. I beg your forgiveness for my inattention. There should never have been a moment when I was unaware of your presence. I should have done everything in my power to ensure you could walk as you wish unharassed. Instead, I indulged in a scuffle with my fellow cadets. I am a disgrace to myself. To the Academy. And most of all to you. I beg for forgiveness I do not deserve and surrender myself fully to your judgment."

You have got to be fucking kidding me.

Fortunately, I keep that thought to myself—just barely—as the other kneeling vamps all take turns repeating some variation of that bullshit, each fawning apology ending with a declaration of undeserved forgiveness and unreserved submission.

The demifae, at least, just stand at attention without moving.

Waiting a moment until after the last of the demivamps grovels, Victor ensures that no one has anything more to add before washing us all with the same angry glare. "You've all disgraced yourselves today," he says, walking to loom over the fae. "You four. Find Commander Asher and inform him of what happened. Two lashes apiece, plus whatever else he believes appropriate."

Wayne the Wolverine's face blanches, the memory of Ellis's whipping still fresh in all our minds, and the demifae suddenly trip over themselves with "yes, sirs" before scurrying off with proverbial tails tucked between their legs.

My stomach tight and pulse pounding, I wait for what Victor has in store for the rest of us.

The count's attention focuses on me, though he speaks to the group. "All apologies have been accepted, and forgiveness is granted," he says, a cold smile touching his face once more. "Samantha. It was…a pleasure to make your acquaintance again. I look forward to seeing you blossom as your education continues." He waves a perfectly manicured hand, the long nails making my skin crawl. "Now, I suggest you visit the infirmary for that nasty little cut. And change into presentable clothes, all of you. This is an academy, not a pigsty."

The demivamps scramble, and I'm smart enough to go right along with them—though I'm not sure whether it's Victor's or Reese's hard glare that I'm truly trying to flee.

3

Reese

*W*ell, *that was a bloody mess.* Reese felt a muscle tic on the side of his jaw as he followed Victor back across the green, but he quickly tamped it down. After a thousand years on Earth, Victor saw all too much—if you let him.

The beautiful little witch had a mouth on her, but a great deal of that impertinence was based in mere ignorance. She had blanched at the demifae cadets' sentence—and had no idea that she'd been risking far worse when she looked Victor in the eye. When she spoke back to him so boldly. Would she have held her tongue if she had? Reese bloody well hoped so, though something inside him whispered that he knew better.

And he hated how much that bothered him.

His hands tightened behind his back, though his face remained even. On the surface, Victor had handled the problem with respect to vampiric protocol—taking formal apologies into account before doling out sentences—but the nuances would be lost on the cadets. The demifae were punished, and the demivamps were not.

Never mind that after one week with Victor in charge, the demifae and demivampires were already scuffling on the damn green. Asher's approach of keeping everyone too busy to brawl came from his navy days, and there was no better proof of concept than seeing what happened when the reins were eased.

Except Victor wasn't just easing the reins, he was giving the demis just enough leather to hang themselves with. It was calculated. Everything the count did was.

"Reesand." Victor turned toward him, and Reese dropped his gaze politely to the ground. The vampiric equivalent of offering a salute to a superior officer.

"Yes, Your Excellence?" Whatever had compelled Victor to insist that Reese accompany him on this stroll, Reese hoped the count would get on with it.

"Ah, so you do remember our manners." Victor flicked his fingers, giving Reese permission to look up. "Tell me, does vampire tradition bother you, Reesand?"

"No." Reese shrugged one shoulder. It really didn't.

"Many powerful families would be glad to welcome you into their folds, yet you appear more comfortable with the mortal species," Victor said smoothly, his sharp features arranged into fatherly concern—some new act the count was apparently trying on for size. "I thought you might have rejected our traditions. It does happen."

"I have no feelings about tradition one way or the other, Your Excellence." Reese had no feelings on most things nowadays. And he liked it that way. "My family was killed during the fae-vampire wars. I am simply not ready to join— or start—another family. Shedding a mortal persona every few years suits my needs."

"No roots. No responsibilities. No place to call home." Victor glanced at him with a small *tsk* sound. "Most would call that unhealthy."

Reese stayed silent. There was nothing to gain by challenging the count. Sometimes victory was best achieved by not getting into the wrong fight at the wrong time.

"Is Cassis not your family, though?" Victor said lightly, straightening a perfectly straight jacket cuff. "I was under the impression your sires were related."

"They were brother and sister. Humans would call us cousins of a sort."

"I would call you brothers." Victor's voice hardened. "Brothers or nothing at all. Those are our ways."

Again, Reese held his tongue. Several oceans could fit between Victor's and his notions of ways.

The light drizzle was turning into a steady rain again, though Victor seemed perfectly at ease. The moisture slicked his dark hair into lustrous strands, making his bottomless black eyes shine brighter. The green had finally emptied around them, all the students closed up in the dining hall for lunch.

"And the witch?" Victor's casual tone sent a ping of warning down Reese's spine. He had the unmistakable sense that they'd just come to the heart of the conversation. And there was nowhere he wanted to be less. "What do you make of Ms. Samantha Devinee?"

"She was caught between two unfriendly forces today, Your Excellence," said Reese.

"True. Being caught in a crossfire between vampire and fae is no way for a young girl to grow and thrive. Yet there is the rub. All the creatures are powerful, each in their own way. And with that power comes the need for discipline. We vampires have our protocol, enforced by our clans. The fae have theirs, which pack leaders teach and enforce among their own. But there are no covens to teach Ms. Devinee her place, not anymore. Do you see where I'm heading with this, Reesand?"

"No, sir."

Victor's eyes flashed, but the show of displeasure was wasted on Reese. The count's power meant that few things in vampire society happened without his blessing—but Reese needed nothing from that world. Victor was his current commanding officer as dean of Talonswood Reform, and it was no more than that. A fleeting arrangement in an immortal's life span.

"Then I shall be straightforward," Victor said dryly. "I've decided that while she is under my command as dean, Samantha would do well to learn vampiric protocol. And it is my wish that you instruct her in it."

Reese stopped dead. "Witches have never followed our protocols, sir."

Unlike the vampires, who defined hierarchy through lineage, or fae, who challenged each other for alpha roles, witch covens had elected their leadership. A slow, unwieldy process involving a great deal more democracy than Reese thought practical, yet he couldn't deny that when a coven of witches *did* make a decision, they were a force to be reckoned with.

"Quite correct," said Victor. "And it got them killed, and nearly dragged the rest of us down too. Samantha is the first witch we've found in a long time, and I refuse to see her follow in their footsteps. She needs a firmer hand. Her magical temper tantrum last week should never have been permitted."

Right. Much better to have had Quinn rape the girl. And the fact that she would one day take one of three empty witch council seats surely had nothing to do with Victor's calculation.

King Bryant had made his claim clear when he sent his

bastard son to Talonswood to keep an eye on the witch. Count Victor was merely asserting his own claim now—and Reese couldn't imagine Bryant would take the challenge lying down. To them, the girl was a pawn on the chessboard. A pawn they both secretly feared was actually the queen.

Men in power were so predictable—Reese had seen it time and again over the centuries, fought for those men in war after war. It was practically boring by now.

His voice hardened. "Let me be clear. Are you ordering me to force Samantha to obey vampiric protocols?" *Because I'd love to know what the council will have to say about that.*

"I'm not ordering you to do anything, Reesand." Victor smiled, his white canines flashing in the afternoon light. "I'm merely informing you of my preferences."

"Yes, sir," Reese said, bowing as Victor dismissed him with a flick of a hand. The count could have saved his breath on the whole *will no one rid me of this meddlesome priest* angle. Hard as it was for Victor to believe, Reese truly needed nothing from the damn count. Certainly nothing over which Reese was going to get any closer to Samantha Devinee than being on an island required. Especially after Ellis and his mating talk.

4

Reese

*W*alking back into the infirmary a half hour later, Reese stopped short in the doorway, the rain water draining from his hair and clothes dripping a puddle on the floor.

"What are you doing here?" he asked dumbly.

The little witch stood up from a waiting chair and looked at him as if he were crazy. She'd changed into leggings and a tiny blue sweatshirt, her damp red hair loose around her face.

"Well?" Reese demanded. The stroll in the rain had barely cooled his temper after observing the efficiency with which Victor was destroying all the progress Asher had spent years building, and he had absolutely zero patience left for a convoluted witch.

Finally—speaking slowly as if English were his second language—the witch deigned to answer. "I hit my head. Count Victor ordered me to come here. If having sat in this chair satisfies the requirement, I'm more than happy to—"

"It doesn't." He gripped the doorframe so hard, he heard a faint crack in the wood. *Idiot Reesand.* "Go on inside."

Opening the door, Reese tried to ignore Samantha's tight backside as she walked past him and stopped beside the exam table as if requiring further instruction.

"Problem?" Reese asked, walking briskly into the room and grabbing a spare shirt from the hanger in the small closet. The infirmary was closer to the gym than his quarters, and he got into the habit of keeping spare clothes here.

"I wasn't the only one bleeding, sir," said Sam. "Why was I the only one ordered here?"

Turning his back to the witch, Reese pulled off his soggy shirt and replaced it with dry cotton. "I presume you are referring to Wayne's nosebleed—though I imagine all the fae are bleeding by now." Reese turned back, juvenilely pleased to see the witch blanch at the reminder. "Vampires and fae heal faster than witches and humans. We generally leave the decision as to when to seek medical aid to those cadets' discretion."

If his answer implied that he didn't trust the witch to make that decision for herself, so much the better. Patting the table, Reese stepped away while the witch swung herself up onto it, her full breasts swaying beneath her shirt in a way that threatened to make the following quarter hour uncomfortable in a whole new way.

Pulling on latex gloves, Reese tilted Sam's head to the side without preamble and peered at the gash on her hairline while the clock on the wall ticked loudly into the silence. Besides her very first day, Reese had never stood this close to the witch before—and he'd never planned to. Now he knew precisely why. He could hear her soft breaths, smell her sweet citrusy scent. See her big hazel eyes tracking his every move. Worse, he could hear the slight pattering of her heartbeat, the smell of her blood making his own heat slightly.

"A few stitches should do it. Are there any parts of your… *fall* you don't fully remember?"

Sam's hands curled around the edge of the table. "I don't like sharps."

"Then don't invite them to your birthday party." Pulling sutures out of their sterile package, Reese laid them out on a drape-covered metal tray before turning to draw lidocaine into a syringe.

What was it with fear of needles lately? First Ellis, now Sam. There must be something in the water.

"I'm not joking." Sam said. Her pallor had already told him she wasn't—which still didn't give her any choice in the matter.

"And I'm not laughing." Reese hardened his voice. Debate and democracy was a witch pastime, not vamps'. "Nor am I asking your opinion. Lie flat."

Moving forward, he put his hands on Sam's shoulders— and nearly jerked back. Hades take him, touching Sam's skin was like brushing against a live wire. Her scent hit him as hard as the undercurrent of fear as she lowered reluctantly to the table.

"For someone who gets this nervous in an infirmary, you certainly get into enough trouble," Reese said, allowing an edge into his words. She had no idea just how much trouble she was inviting onto herself with Victor—and it infuriated Reese how the girl's ignorance worried him. First, it wasn't his problem. And second, one trip to Asher's office and she'd get over her mouthiness efficiently enough.

Samantha inhaled sharply, bringing Reese's attention back to her face. She'd grown paler still, her eyes tightening with fear that now seeped freely into her scent.

He softened his tone. "Easy, Samantha. If I wanted to torture you, I'd forgo the numbing."

No response. No nervous chuckle or caustic comment. Beneath his hands, Sam's pulse echoed through her body, her tight muscles already starting to shake.

Reese hesitated, his brows tightened in uncertainty. There was nervous, and then there was this. Downright terrified. And terrified patients were bloody unpredictable.

Indecision played over Reese's conscience, safety winning the morality game after a moment's thought.

"Samantha." Leaning over the shaking girl, he caught her gaze, feeling his own eyes dilate with vampiric compulsion. The warmbloods were all susceptible to the vampires' mental coercion, though the suggestion worked better when the chosen order was something the victim wanted to begin with. Of course the vampire's personal strength mattered too—and Reese was as powerful as Cassis. "You want this over with quickly. Staying still will make that happen, right? That's what you want, isn't it?"

"I want you to go to hell." Sam said through clenched teeth.

This time, Reese did jerk back.

It hadn't worked. The compulsion should have sliced through the witch, but had easily ricocheted from her instead. Worse still was the look on her face. Her eyes flashed once at River, her rich hazel gaze saying she'd seen what he tried to do and hated him for the attempted intrusion, and then…then they unfocused. A blink, and Sam's eyes stared into nothing in a way that Reese had seen in soldiers who never fully returned from a battlefield.

The way he'd seen in Ellis too many times to count when he was having a flashback.

And it finally hit him. Samantha wasn't afraid of needles. Ellis was.

"What do you see in front of you?" Reese whispered gently into Sam's ear.

Her response turned his blood to ice. "Sienna."

5

Sam

𝒲alking into my room a few days after getting *sam-witched* on the green, I nearly trip over my own feet at the sight of a slim girl sitting on what used to be Bernadette's bed. With her black hair in a spiky bob and a dusting of freckles across the bridge of her nose, the girl's delicate features make her look pixie-like. Her legs are drawn up, a small, very expensive laptop balancing on her knees.

"Who are you?" I ask, crossing my arms over my white uniform blouse.

The girl lifts her chin, the hopeful look in her large brown eyes making me think she knows little about the joys of Talonswood Reform. "I'm Mika. I'm… It's my first day, and this is where they put me."

Did they now?

"Sam." I toss my books onto my desk, instinctively checking to ensure everything is still as I left it—it is. In addition to a letter with my name on it, still sealed. Tearing

29

open the envelope, I scan the unfamiliar handwriting, learning that somehow, Cassis's request that I continue to work off my debt by bartending during liberty days has been approved. My jaw clenches. Just when I thought the Academy's draconian rules were going to work in my favor for once, they twist them on me.

Realizing that Mika is still looking at me expectantly, I sigh and turn to her. "Look, in case no one's told you, I'm a witch. And that makes me the last person you want to be seen with around here."

Mika snorts. "I'm a computer geek. I gave up trying to be popular back in middle school. If someone really annoyed me, I'd just change their grades." She swipes her bangs from her face, but they fall right back over her eyes. "Commander Asher did tell me about you, though. I've always wanted to meet a witch, but you aren't exactly an easy find. Well, you know." She shrugs. "So what got you sent here?"

Ellis. My chest clenches again, and I have to fight to shut down the storm of emotions his name sends through me. I still haven't had a chance to talk to him—which seems remarkably unfair given that he's still sharing his flashbacks of Sienna with me. Yesterday, I saw him eating alone in a corner of the dining hall, but when I started toward him, he pushed away his tray and full-on shifted into his huge white wolf to avoid me. Yeah. That one stung. Then again, I got him whipped halfway to death, so it's not as if he's lacking reasons to dislike me—just in case the fact that the last witch he was around captured and tortured him for a decade wasn't enough of one.

Realizing that Mika's large eyes are now shifting to concern, I quickly wipe the emotion from my face. "I made a deal with a fae male before I knew this whole other world existed. Burglarized the wrong house for the right thing." I push back another pang, the memory of the ruby calling out to me brushing something deep inside my chest. "Long story short, I got caught and sent to this prison. Listen, my last roommate tried to murder me. So don't expect us to—" I stop talking as Mika's fingers fly over her keyboard. Writing down our conversation like a court stenographer? "What the hell are you doing?"

Silence.

Mika blinks, looking up in surprise as if she just realized no more words are coming from my mouth. "Oh. Sorry." Her nose crinkles as she makes an apologetic face. "I was checking the network. It's a nervous habit, and with the wet welcome and you talking about murder and prison…" She touches her still-drying hair and shudders.

Shit. I don't know how I managed to forget the welcome hosing, but plainly, Mika had just enjoyed the same one. The memory of Asher and Reese just standing there and watching sends a shiver down my spine, replaced by a surge of heat as I remember Ellis stripping beside me, revealing his exquisitely muscled body inch by inch.

Clearing my throat, I try to divert attention from my blush by nodding my chin toward Mika's laptop. "Talonswood blocks transmissions, by the way, so even cell phones don't call beyond the island. So if you think you'll be getting online anytime—" I freeze as the opening credits from *South Park* fill the room.

"I hope you like *Adult Swim*," Mika says, tapping away. "I'm a bit addicted. That and sci-fi. Have you seen *Battlestar Galactica*? Oh, and *Buffy the Vampire Slayer*. Not sci-fi and kind of ironic given where we are, but I won't be able to help myself."

"How… How the hell did you manage that?"

"Hacked my way through the security net. It's not that there's no service here, it's just that the great powers that be think they can block it. Let me tell you, there's a big difference between what people think they can do and what they can actually do. I think the same geniuses that set up the cyber wall also installed those locks there." She motions toward the electronic mechanism on the door that turns Talonswood's dorm rooms into actual jail, the red light now blinking for curfew.

Mika's hands fly across her keyboard, and the red light blinks to green before turning red again. Then green. Then... green green red, green green red, green green green green greeeeeen.

"Fuck me." I swallow. "Did you just make the locks play 'Jingle Bells'?"

Mika grins, her impish smile transforming her face into a fountain of mischief that makes it very difficult not to like her. "It was the first song to come to mind. I have no ear for music. Anyway, you were telling me how you got here."

"Were you actually listening?" I ask.

"Oh... Um. No. Sorry." She bites her lip. "I started hacking, and it kinda took over. Which is basically what got me here to begin with. I hacked into the Pentagon, and then one thing led to another...and... Well, they made it very difficult for me to say no to coming here, if you know what I mean." For the first time, her voice falters, and she blinks too quickly several times before conjuring up a brave smile. "The trip from San Francisco was a bitch. Not that I remember any of it. Do you even know what continent we're on?" She looks around as if our small white-walled dorm room might hold some clues.

"No, but my guess is Europe. Well, it's an island, but I think Europe is the closest continent." I walk over to my dresser, pulling out a pair of sweats to trade for the uniform skirt. "So are you fae or vamp?" I ask over my shoulder. I think vamp, given her pale skin, but it's also possible that my new roommate just never realized there *was* a sun outside.

"Oh, vamp. I'm lucky that way. Not that it's not lucky to be a witch," she clarifies quickly. "I mean I'm lucky that I've always *known* I'm part vamp, so no huge shock to learn that I'm not human or about Talonswood or fae or anything. Except the part where I got sent here. That was a shock." Mika pauses, biting her nail, the temporary quiet in the room already feeling like a rare commodity.

"It's all right. You don't have to tell me." I try to sound reassuring. Mika is like a bouncy puppy, and I don't want to see her hurt.

"It's not like it's a secret," she says, though her shoulders curl in a bit as she speaks. Under her neon-yellow hoody, I can see that she's tiny, almost birdlike. If she weren't a vamp, I'd be as worried for her at combat training as I am for myself. "I got cocky, that's the bottom line. But, in my defense, I was racing against the clock. It was a competition on the dark web, and I won it last year. But then they were patching just at the wrong time, and, well, the rest is history. Sorry. I'm talking too much again." A small blush touches her pale skin, her large eyes failing to hide heart-wrenching hope. "I just want you to like me."

I do. Unfortunately. She reminds me of Janie, and it's kind of heartbreaking how easily that gets past my carefully built defenses.

"Look, Mika." I make my voice kind, but with a sort of steel underneath that lets her know I'm not fucking around. "I'm a witch and about the least popular person in the entire Academy. The best thing you can do is not be seen with me. Ever. In fact, if you need to shove me in the hallway or something to keep yourself from getting your ass kicked, I understand. Just know that I'll shove back."

Mike frowns at me over her laptop screen as if she's no longer certain I'm all there. "Hello. Earth to Samantha. Have you met me? Because computer nerds and cool kids go together about as well as, well, vamps and fae at a hunting competition. So if it's all the same to you, I'll pick my roommate's friendship over theirs."

"Your funeral." I shake my head, unable to keep my gaze from sliding to the red light on the door. Ellis must be in his room now. Walking over to the door, I try the lock, though I know it's useless. No give.

I've even tried drawing that opening spell rune that Ellis taught me when we were locked in the cage. But either I'm doing it wrong or my magic is on vacation, or who knows why, but it didn't work. And my old lock-picking skills are no good with the high-tech stuff either—beating high-end locks isn't a skill that's exactly in high demand in the slums where I worked.

"I can open it for you," Mika says. "Just say the word."

I frown at her. "You can?"

"Pfft." her bangs flop a little when she makes the sound. "I mean, *Jingle Bells.*' It's not exactly difficult."

Well, now. A small grin touches my face. "Can you open other rooms too?"

Mika's grin widens. "A challenge? *Now* we're talking. Give me the number, and I'll deliver Christmas."

6

Sam

$\mathcal{M}$y heart pounds as I push open the door, half expecting an alarm to go off with guards flooding the hallway. But there's nothing but silence, the floor that we regularly spent half a day hand-waxing under Asher's rule reflecting the pale wall sconces. Crossing quickly to Ellis's room, I pause for a moment, suddenly unsure whether I should knock or just let myself in. I mean knocking is akin to asking for permission, and I'm through asking. If Ellis is going to turn his back—or his tail—on me, I want a conversation. Whether I deserve one or not. Drawing a final breath of courage, I push down on the handle—and stop at the sound of voices coming from inside the room.

"Reese says you aren't healing." Asher's voice. Fuck.

I start to back away, but freeze when the words penetrate.

"Reese talks too much." The strain in Ellis's voice churns my stomach because I know it's my fault. Ellis growls softly. "I don't trust Victor, Ash. Not with Sam—"

"The witch has been nothing but trouble since she showed up," Asher snarls. "And it's only going to get worse."

I step back, and the door handle snaps as I release it, the click deafeningly loud in the empty hall. Shit. My breath halts as the voices in Ellis's room stop abruptly. I shoot a glance at my own door, take a step back and—

Ellis's door swings open, Asher filling the frame. He steps out when he sees me, his tawny eyes and heady sandalwood scent pinning me in place. Straightened to his full towering height and standing so close to me, the male is intimidating as hell. And just as hot, with his mane of golden hair and smoothly carved features. He's dressed less formally than usual in slim jeans and a moss-green Henley that hugs every hard ridge of his pecs and abs.

"What are you doing here, Devinee?" His low voice sends a shiver down my spine.

"I wanted to check on Ellis, sir." I clear my throat, following Asher's glance to the lock, glowing with green light. My thready pulse taps in my throat, but I raise my chin anyway.

Asher frowns, a muscle in his jaw twitching as he no doubt tries to work out how and why the system malfunctioned.

Not one to let a good cover go to waste, I press on shamelessly. "I thought that since the doors were open—"

"Go back to yer room, Devinee." Ellis's gravelly Scottish voice comes from behind Asher, and I peer around so I can see him.

The male sits shirtless on the edge of his bed, hunched over with his elbows braced on his knees. His light blond hair is tied back in a knot, bandages wrapped around his torso and shoulders. My heart stops with the need to touch him, to reassure myself that he's all right. Except he isn't. Though his voice sounded firm, there's a pallor to his skin, a tightness to his golden eyes that speaks of pain.

I take a step toward him.

Asher blocks my path, his nostrils flaring. Does he think Ellis needs to be protected from me? That I'm too much trouble to let near his brother?

"I can help." My voice has a strength I don't feel but can fake well. "Ellis. Listen to me. There was iron on that whip." Despite my best judgment, I cut a vicious glance at the asshole who wielded it, getting savage pleasure from seeing Asher's face tighten. "I can pull it from your blood, just like when—"

"Get the hell out of my room." Ellis's voice snaps like the whip that struck him, my heart recoiling at the sting. "I don't want you here."

I swallow the lump of hurt and confusion, trying desperately to comprehend his reasoning. I get needing time to recover after what we went through, after what happened with Quinn. I even get wanting to keep his distance from me. But this? He doesn't just seem distant—he seems hostile.

"I don't understand." I step quickly around Asher to face Ellis head-on. There was something between us back in that cage, a connection so fierce that it gripped my soul and magic both. That it still sends me nightmare postcards each evening. A bond that must still be there, because it's too strong not to be. "I just want to talk. To tell you I'm sorry about—"

"Ellis asked that you leave." Asher's beautiful face is as hard as granite as he shifts his weight to stand between his brother and me. When he speaks, there's no mistaking the note of command—the promise of punishment if I don't comply. "That's reason enough for you to turn around and walk back to your room."

At the edge of my vision, I see Ellis's forehead tense, but

when I look at him directly, that hesitation is gone. The male's golden eyes flash at me. *Go away.*

What the hell? For a moment, I just stand there as if waiting for some curtain to lift, to reveal a different reality.

But it doesn't. And Ellis's gaze doesn't warm either.

"Right." I step back, as if space might save me from the bruising force of Ellis's fire and ice. Whatever happened, whatever changed between Ellis and me to make him hate me so much, I need to get as far away from it as possible. "I shouldn't have come."

"No, you shouldn't have," Ellis confirms, and fuck me if that doesn't hurt.

Boxing me out with his body, Asher jerks his chin toward the hallway. "Go. You're supposed to be in your room, Samantha. A malfunctioning lock isn't permission to do as you please."

I'm numb as I turn my back to Ellis and walk out, Asher following on my heels.

"How long were you out here?" the male asks coolly, his words striking me between the shoulder blades.

I pause. Draw breath. Tell my stinging eyes to shove any thoughts of tears up their ass, and let the slow simmer of anger spill into my blood. "Long enough to know that *the witch* brought trouble with her."

Asher exhales behind me. "Samantha—"

I must be suicidal, because I speed up as if I didn't hear him. Maybe I don't care. Maybe I want to piss Asher off. I don't know.

He moves faster than I can track, a streak of warm muscle that overtakes me and pins me to the wall, one hard arm on either side of my shoulders. A small rumbling growl escapes his chest, the wolf inside him closer to the surface than I've ever seen in the controlled military asshole.

38

"Is this the part where you threaten to take a whip to me as well, sir?" I say, which is stupid but comes out of my mouth anyway.

"This is the part where I tell you to pull your head out of your ass," Asher snaps, the heat of his fury rolling off him in waves. "Though whipping you might actually do some good." He draws a breath, the effort of keeping himself in check seeming to consume his attention for several heartbeats. "You are new to our world, Samantha, but the carte blanche your ignorance is granting you is running out much faster than you think. That bullshit about being confused over the open door? Lose it. You and I both know you knew the rules."

Yeah, well, can't really argue with that one.

Meeting his gaze, I stay silent. Not meek, but silent. The male's earthy sandalwood scent pins me in place as firmly as his hands.

"Do not press Count Victor," Asher says, enunciating each word. "Do not press me. And for fuck's sake, do not press Ellis. Do you understand?"

Instead of answering, I reach for my magic, trying to imagine something happening. The earth opening up and swallowing him whole, for instance. Or swallowing me. Neither condescends to happen. I haven't felt that buzzing in my blood since the day Quinn trapped me in my room.

"Cadet?" Asher prompts.

"Yes, sir." I mean the words to sound empty, but they are not. They hurt. "I understand."

7

Asher

*a*sher's hand tightened around his drink as he watched a group of demivamps take body shots off a female cadet. The girl laughed and writhed beneath them, shirt pulled up to her bra, aware of every male gaze in the room. Dusk's pounding electronic music was giving him a headache—or maybe it was the shrieks of newly liberated demis grinding against each other on the dance floor, the weekend stretching out blissfully before them.

Not only were the cadets descending into the very debauchery and creature rivalry Talonswood Reform had been founded to rein in, but Victor was all but cheering them on—while Sam attracted trouble like some kind of nuclear magnet. How the hell was Asher supposed to keep the cadets in check when the unholy duo of Count Victor and Samantha Devinee outflanked him on all sides?

In seeming mockery of that thought, Samantha stepped out quietly from behind the bar to deliver an order, obviously doing everything she could to avoid being looked at. It wasn't working. In her skintight black jeans and tank top, red-streaked hair swinging against her shoulders, she looked breathtaking. Ethereal. Dusk's low red-tinted light sharpened her cheekbones and drew deep shadows beneath them. She was doing wonders for Cassis's business already, every male vamp in the room seeming magnetically drawn to the bar, exuding a mixture of lust, hate, and fascination that made Asher's skin crawl.

Everything about Sam made his skin crawl, actually, his damn body lusting after the delicious witch even as he longed to get her gone from his academy. From the whole damn island. That, however, was impossible. Bryant had brought Samantha to Talonswood in hopes of making the witch malleable to his will, and Victor plainly had the same thought in mind. It wasn't Samantha's fault that she was caught in a surrogate war between two manipulative bastards, but fault little mattered. What mattered was the bottom line: everything Asher had ever worked for, fae and vamps coexisting without bloodshed, the witch was putting in jeopardy just by existing.

"Earth to Asher," Reese said, tapping the table in front of Asher. Dressed in a pair of jeans and a black button-down shirt with the sleeves rolled up to expose corded forearms, the vampire had his customary brooding darkness settled around him. "Where'd you go, warmblood? We're discussing Ellis's absurd little theory."

Asher rubbed the spot on his inner forearm where Sienna had left the same mark Ellis had over his heart and Cassis wore on his shoulder blade. Reese's mark, also on the forearm, was covered beneath a Celtic knot tattoo that he had to re-ink every few months.

"Ellis's theory?" Asher kept his voice low, though, given the din around them, no one was likely to overhear even if he shouted. "You mean that we all, Cassis included, are fated mates to a witch? Don't tell me you think it's true."

"Of course not." Reese's mouth twisted as if the mere suggestion of a connection was too outlandish to contemplate. In fairness, since Sienna tore away his wife, the vamp had only survived by letting no one else get close. Unlike most normal beings, Reese had no middle ground. He either didn't give a fuck, or he gave far too many.

"Bollocks, bloodsucker. You feel a pull." Ellis leaned toward Reese. "Look me in the eye and tell me you don't."

Asher's chest tightened, a shot of unwelcome anxiety spilling into his blood as he awaited the vamp's answer.

Reese took a sip of whiskey and met Ellis's gaze. "I feel a pull to strangle her, but I think magic has nothing to do with it."

Right. Reese was right.

"There's something there," Ellis growled from his shadowy corner. "She saw Sienna in my memories when the marks connected. Now she's seeing Sienna when we're not even connected." The male shook his head. "There has to be a way to put a stop to that."

Leaning back in his chair, Asher watched the injured warrior silently. Though Ellis had flatly told Asher exactly which hell to go to when he'd tried to inquire about the wounds, the male's scent hinted at the iron poisoning Reese feared. And if the beads of sweat along Ellis's hairline were any indication, he was running a fever to boot.

"Here you are. O negative." Appearing with a tray beside Reese, Samantha set a silver goblet in front of him. Despite the polite tone, the girl was holding her breath, and Reese moved the blood to the other side of the table.

"Thank you," he said.

Sam nodded without looking at him. "And here is the ale

you—" Her words faltered, her body stiffening as she noticed Ellis's presence. The drink Sam was about to place before Asher hung tensely in the air, her hand tight around the frosted glass. "Hello."

Ellis nodded curtly.

Sam's hand tightened around her glass, the only sign of feeling anything the little witch was willing to show. "Is there anything I can get for you?" Sam asked, her voice so collected that it could only be an act.

"Aye. Privacy." Turning to Reese, Ellis asked him something about mid-twentieth-century military strategy, leaving Sam the choice of either listening to Reese's account of the Korean War or scurrying off like the bloody hired help.

Taking his glass out of the witch's hand, Asher thanked her quietly and watched her walk back to the bar, tension lining the delicate muscles of her neck and shoulders.

For an absurd second, Asher felt the urge to drive a fist into Ellis's nose. Sam might be a witch, but she was a cadet under Asher's care, and that made him responsible for her. Yes, that was why Asher's voice came out in a low growl. "Was that necessary?"

Ellis met Asher's hard gaze without flinching, his eyes glassy with a mix of fever and pain. "I chose to do it, didn't I?" he shook himself. "Did you miss the part where she's having *my* damn flashbacks, feeling *my* pain? The less contact she has with me, the better."

"She still deserves to be treated with the courtesy due a…" Asher stopped speaking. Due a what? A mate? A lover? None of those things were Asher's business. If he was taking no one into his life, what right did he have to fault Ellis for doing the same? "Forget it. I'm not getting involved in a tiff between *two cadets.*"

Ellis snorted. "Yeah. That's all she is to you. All we both are."

Asher shook his head, grateful that Cassis chose that moment to settle behind the grand piano and start a haunting Rachmaninov piece, the notes soul shattering beneath the male's fingers. It was the kind of music that could make you forget anything, even the vampire and witch who were bringing the world down around your ears.

"Fuck me." Reese glared at the door. "To what do we owe this pleasure?"

Dragging his attention back to the table, Asher followed Reese's comment and gaze toward the door, where Count Victor and his entourage were striding into the club. In a tailored gray Armani suit, snow-white shirt, and a tie to match the blackness of his hair and soul, Victor reminded Asher of a mob boss of old. Except infinitely more dangerous.

It took all of three warm heartbeats for Dusk's patrons to recognize the presence of greatness in their midst and part like the Red Sea before Victor's feet. Technically speaking, outside of an official event, only vampires beneath Victor's direct command were required to show him deference. But many, many others chose to regardless. And just as he'd done with the Academy's cadets, Victor drank in every drop of subservience, taking stock of which females knelt before him, which males lowered their gazes. And which ones did not.

Cassis, being Cassis, started playing a crude jig, dark eyes flashing with a suicidal mirth.

At the bar, Sam was so engrossed in Cassis's music, Asher wagered she hadn't even noticed the change in atmosphere until the whole place had shifted. When she finally managed to tear her attention away from the piano to find Victor presiding over a dozen kneeling and bowed vamps, the witch waved at him cheerily.

Asher's stomach clenched.

"Count Victor. Good evening," Sam called, her musical soprano loud and clear as she met Victor's eyes with all the brashness of an equal. "What can I get started for you?"

Beside Asher, Reese stood up as silently as a sniper from his nest, tension lining every muscle in his body.

Victor flicked his hand at the courtiers, never taking his dark eyes off Sam, and the bar returned haltingly to its evening. An illusion that Asher doubted would be long-lived.

"Martini," Victor answered curtly, just loud enough to be heard over Cassis's playing, before turning to look right at Reese. "The blood kind."

As Asher watched, something passed between them. Reese lowered his gaze, as his position beneath Victor's official command required. Perfectly appropriate and polite.

"Is there going to be trouble?" Asher asked quietly.

"I don't know." Reese jerked his chin at Ellis. "Get him out of here."

A small growl escaped Ellis's chest, and Asher, who'd been about to close his hand around the male's bicep, pulled back at once. Ellis might be a cadet at Talonswood, but here and now, with his mate in Victor's crosshairs, he would rip Asher's head off without blinking. They all knew it.

Just as Asher knew that Ellis's protective instincts were the last thing this situation needed. As were Asher's own.

8

Sam

*a*dding Victor's blood martini to the list of orders, I cling to the sound of Cassis's music. His long fingers fly over the piano keys, a cocky look on his shadowed face making the notes into the grandest fuck-you to the universe I've ever heard. Louise—yes, the vamp named his piano—responds beautifully to Cassis's touch, making the music fill my soul with color despite the three males sitting at the back of Dusk. Ellis. Asher. Reese.

Don't look. Don't feel. Keep pouring drinks.

That part's easy enough. I've tended bar before—and slimy creeps are the same no matter where you go. Only difference is these ones have fangs. Despite being open to all, Dusk is very much a vamp-centered pleasure hole—though a very high-end one.

Not that the gaggle of shot-downing cadets lacks money to pay.

I resist the urge to tug up my neckline, knowing it will only draw more attention to my breasts—this is one of only two presentable tank tops I own, and it's about five years too small for me. The other one, my white cami, still has bloodstains on it from the last time I came here and nearly caused a riot.

I smile at the few regulars sitting at the long semicircular bar. The vamps nod back by way of greeting. Not what you'd call warm, but not hostile either, which in my case is a plus. Especially given the demi entourage Victor brought with him. Devin and Leanna are now actually kneeling at the count's feet as he lights up a cigar.

To each their own.

I still don't know why Victor is allowing cadets to go into town on liberty days. Maybe the rule was just so poorly enforced, he didn't see a reason to continue pretending it existed, or else he enjoys the demis slinking faithfully by his side the whole time.

Or he's hoping we'll stray into the woods and get killed by something.

Reading through the next order, I pull a silver goblet off the rack and go about the mixing. It took me a bit of time to learn the preferences of Cassis's patrons—from the "standard" drinks with alcohol so expensive that my hands shook the first few times I handled the bottles, to the specialty cocktails made with blood kept in silver-and-glass decanters, each carefully labeled with the name of the creature it came from. *Jasmine Ford, twenty-three.*

This kind of drink still makes my stomach turn.

"Well, this is nice, a witch serving up like she should," a crooked-nosed vamp says, sliding up to the bar. "I was wondering why Cassis brought you, but it finally clicked. What other services do you offer, luv? I could think of a thing or two for that pretty mouth to get busy with."

"As could I, but alas, the lady is occupied." Leaning both elbows against the bar, Cassis flashes a fang-filled smile at the filth, his smooth British accent perfectly polite. "Plus, I don't like to share."

"Yes, you do," the vamp says. "But I didn't know she was yours, Cas."

I didn't either.

Cassis shrugs, leaning over the bar to pour himself a glass of his favorite whiskey. I try not to watch him too closely. With his high cheekbones, sharp jaw, and full lips, he's too beautiful for normal life. He belongs in a Renaissance painting. He's wearing one of his Versace suits again, the tight midnight-blue jacket and pants fitting perfectly over his tall, lean frame. The fresh shampoo scent of his dark hair brushes my nose, waking my body to his presence as intensely as his music did.

I stomp down the misplaced arousal. Cassis isn't interested, and I was the biggest idiot in the universe to think otherwise.

"Why do you really have me here?" I ask Cassis as crooked nose waddles off to find himself a new girl to seduce. "And don't tell me it's to pay off a bill."

Cassis winks, which is not a satisfactory answer at all. "Let me know if anyone else bothers you. Given our company this evening, they might."

"Why do they—you—all dislike witches?" I ask. The hatred coming from the vamps around Victor's table is growing more palpable by the heartbeat.

"The same reason everyone dislikes things," says Cassis, shrugging one broad shoulder. "Witches were powerful once and never let the others forget it. The hubris got them exposed to humans at the end, and we all know how that turned out. A cautionary tale for creatures everywhere, and you, Samantha, are a walking warm-blooded reminder."

The way Cassis says *blood* sends a shiver down my spine, my skin prickling with the memory of his teeth sinking into my neck. I should be frightened. Instead, I'm getting damp.

Cassis cocks a brow. Yes, of course the asshole smells it.

I flip him off, and he laughs—which, of course, just makes him more distractingly beautiful, his white teeth flashing between deep smile creases, fangs sheathed for my benefit.

"So is there a Dusk equivalent for the fae somewhere on the island?" I ask, desperate to change the topic.

"There is no Dusk equivalent anywhere, Samantha," Cassis purrs. "But if you mean why are there so many more vamps than fae around, it's because the Talon gateway is just three blocks north—unless they have some business in the mortal world, most of the fae slink off to Talon the first chance they get. Think of it as their own little world-cave. Vampires, on the other hand, have always dwelt among humans. Do you know why?"

"No."

Cassis leans closer, his dark, eternal eyes dancing with amusement. "This is where the food is."

I shove him, though there is no actually moving the muscular shoulder. But it gets my point across. "Stop being dramatic, Dracula. I haven't seen you kill anyone."

"I haven't seen you use the toilet. That doesn't mean you don't." Cassis settles his drink back on the bar.

"Funny."

Selena Gomez's latest hit comes on through Cassis's world-class speakers, and the male closes his eyes for a moment in pleasure, a small smile curling his lips. "These modern bards. Not too bad for warmbloods, wouldn't you say?"

I roll my eyes and turn back to my work. Pouring Victor's martini into a glass, I settle it onto my tray and map my route through the room to avoid coming within eye-contact range of the dark trio in the back. If the fact that I'd rather serve Count Victor than Ellis doesn't send the message about just how little I appreciate his attitude, I don't know what will.

Straightening my spine, I walk over to Victor's table. The intensity with which he watches me approach makes my skin crawl. I can't figure the vamp out, what he wants from me—though I'm sure it's something. I shake off the thought. At the moment, I know exactly what he wants—the drink he asked for.

Navigating around the vamps and demis who are clustered around Victor as if he's a cross of the Godfather and Cleopatra, I take the blood martini off my tray. "Here you are, s—" The small tap of Christian's hip against my elbow could be called accidental in another world, but now it just slows time in breathless horror.

My hand buckles.

My tray falls.

The drink in my fingers slips into the air, the thick red liquid flying like something from a laundry detergent commercial, hitting the middle of the count's expensive white shirt with sniper precision.

Shit.

I stare at the mess, my eyes wide. In the corner of my eye, I see Christian cross his arms and stare, as if he had nothing to do with the accident. Well, it's not as if I actually expected him to own up.

"I am so sorry," I tell Count Victor, reaching for the towel tucked into my belt, without quite knowing what to do with it.

Voices have lowered to a whisper across the club. Even in the red-lit shadows, I can feel their faces turned toward me—toward the show.

Victor looks down at his shirt, then lifts his sharp face toward me, cold and deeply shadowed. Waiting. Expecting something. "Are you?" he inquires after a heartbeat, his voice too loud to be casual.

"Of course." I blink. Does he think I orchestrated this?

With the attention of the entire club on me now, my heart is pounding, my raised chin a matter of trained posture. No matter what I feel inside, if I've learned anything in my life, it's never to let fear show. Fear is like blood in the water to sharks.

"Then perhaps you should reconsider the manner in which you are choosing to express your regrets, Samantha," says Victor, his Romanian accent crisp and clear. Behind his left shoulder, Leanne smiles, fangs elongating slowly when she knows I'm looking.

That pregnant silence settles between us again, the count's gaze flickering—of all places—to the back of the room, where Reese, Ellis, and Asher are sitting. As if the answer is somewhere there.

"Beg forgiveness on your knees," Christian instructs, uncrossing his arms to step up to Victor's side. Gold skull-and-cross-bone cuff links flash at his wrists. "*That* is how a low one like you apologizes to the count. And you don't look a master in the eye. You haven't earned the privilege, *witch*."

"Master?" Cassis's smooth voice comes up behind me, making me realize the music has stopped, the temperature in the room dipping once more. Brushing his gaze lazily over Christian, Leanna, and the rest of the entourage, Cassis returns his attention to the count. "I see you are adopting strays, Victor. Very nice. Mazel tov. Given that Dusk is not a wildlife shelter, however, perhaps you and your new pets might find amusement elsewhere."

Victor leans back in his chair, his hand flicking over the wet stain on his shirt. "Your witch has no manners, Cassis."

"Good. That's what I pay her for—just in case you forgot that I'm the ranking vampire in this establishment. *My witch* reports to me." Cassis's gaze cuts to me. "Get back behind the bar, if you please, Samantha."

Confusion grips my body, my thoughts spinning to catch

up. *Beg forgiveness… Ranking vampire.* What in the ever-loving fuck is everyone talking about? I can't begin to detangle the nuances that seem to be passing between Victor and Cassis, but I've a growing understanding that no matter what I do just now, it will piss off someone. Both the males have given me an order, after all, and the two commands are mutually exclusive.

"Now, Devinee," Cassis growls in my ear, making me jump.

Gathering my dignity, I quickly decide in Cassis's favor and add a "Yes, sir," for good measure as I start toward the bar.

One step later, Christian grabs my hair and shoves me down to my knees. Hard.

"Apologize to the count, witch slut," he demands in his guttural French accent. "Show how a proper lowlife greets someone above her station."

I don't see Cassis move until his hand is on Christian's neck and the cadet is up on his toes. "Not in my bar, demi." With a shove of a powerful hand, Cassis tosses Christian halfway across the room, the table the boy lands against cracking to bits. Holy fuck. Straightening his cuff links, Cassis steps between Victor and me. "I don't make a habit of throwing out customers, but you've ruined my drinking plans. Lovely seeing you, Victor. Don't come again."

Silence. Utter, unbroken silence.

I'm just daring to draw a breath when a pair of leather-clad vamps who'd been standing behind the count grab Cassis's arms, a third slamming his fist into Cassis's abdomen.

Cassis takes the blow with a smirk that has his attacker hesitating before drawing a fist back for the next blow. But that one never lands.

With vicious elegance, Cassis wrenches his arms free, the heel of his hand cracking so hard into his assailant that the sound of the male's breaking nose echoes through the room.

The other two goons are dispatched just as quickly, and I take that as my cue to get the hell away.

The moment I start to rise, Leanne backhands me right back to the floor. A ringing sound fills my head. The room swims slightly as I push myself up, a trickle of blood running from my nose down my cheek.

I hear a sharp hiss of breath from multiple corners of the room, the scent of my fresh blood blooming into the air like gasoline in a burning house. Savage growls sound from the back of the room. Asher, Ellis, and Reese are on their feet and moving toward me. To my right, a growing pack of vamps are grabbing bottles and breaking chairs for makeshift clubs, their canines elongated and gleaming under the red lights.

Cassis's eyes narrow at the blood trickling down my face, his pupils dilating. As his fingers curl into a fist, the fury rolling off him spurs my heart into a full-out gallop. With Cassis now squaring off against Victor, the air crackles with tension. The too-quiet room feels like a drawn-back punch, the energy about to release with a deadly force that no one can stop.

Fuck. Fuck. Fuck.

"Stop," says Victor.

And shit. They all do. The vamps put down their weapons, letting their empty hands fall to their sides.

The power this one male has over the world finally hits me.

"Something is breaking tonight, Cassis," Victor says, his voice as calm and measured as if the two are sharing a spot of tea. "But perhaps we are civilized enough to address the problem without collateral damage? At my age, I've learned there is rarely a need to scorch the earth simply to eradicate a single offending weed." Victor puffs on his cigar, the sweet smell of tobacco filling the air.

"Your bartender offended me," he continues. "You unwisely removed her opportunity to apologize, and yet the insult must be set to rights. To this end, I shall give you a choice. Stand aside while the witch is punished, punish her yourself, or bear the penalty on her behalf. As you so eloquently stated, this is your domain, Cassis. It's only tradition that the choice be yours."

Cassis huffs a laugh, opening his arms wide. "Take all the blows on me you want, Victor. I haven't had a good massage in decades."

A corner of Victor's mouth twitches. Then he turns to his minions. "Destroy the piano."

"No," I scream, struggling to my feet. Cassis flinches but holds still, his mouth set in a tight line as an awful, awful sound fills Dusk.

9

Reese

The final soul-piercing moans of piano strings vibrated through Reese as he wrapped up his morning jog, his thoughts as jumbled as they'd been when he started the run. The sun had risen on the first clear, sunny day in over a week, blue sky showing through the forest's dense canopy where a pair of birds currently rioted. The pine-scented trails were calm as always. The same could not be said of Reese's mind, however.

Last night's performance at Dusk had been a setup, a demonstration Victor orchestrated to show Reese the costs of disobeying the count's wishes. Victor could have been no more clear if he'd sent a postcard with *teach Samantha how to grovel properly or I hurt your brother* spelled out in bright red ink.

To the bastard's credit, Victor had hit all the right pressure points. That was the problem with caring for someone—it meant you *had* pressure points. But Cassis was Reese's brother.

As for Samantha… The image of the witch on her knees in the middle of a snarling nest of vamps, the pulsing red light illuminating the blood running down her full lips, it all sent a shiver of inexplicable fury through Reese's soul. Fury that he'd tried—and failed—to run himself free of this morning.

Inside his pocket, his phone vibrated with insistent messages. One of his former commanders from the SEALs, a fellow vamp, ran a private protection force and was busy trying to lure him back into the fold.

Two days ago, he would have called it a nonstarter. He hadn't been gone long enough, and his routine lay with the official militaries. Delta Force was up on his list next, though he might pivot and go to the UK for a stint in the SAS.

But now—now it sounded like relief. A ticket to get the hell away from Victor's manipulations. This clusterfuck of a situation. From a witch who made Reese feel when he didn't want to.

"Running away?" Shifting out of his wolf form, Asher ran a hand through his sweat-soaked golden hair and jerked his chin at the phone that was now in Reese's hand. "Or just running?"

Reese snorted. Of course Asher was trailing him. He'd been at the club last night, saw Victor's little dog and pony show—he would want answers.

"Where do your clothes go when you shift?" Reese shoved his phone back into his pocket. "I never thought to ask."

"Damned if I know." Falling in step beside Reese as they neared the edge of the forest, Asher kept the kind of companionable silence that let you know that he was ready to listen, yet with no pressure to speak before you were ready. It was one of the things that had made him a great general over the centuries. Asher cared about the people under him—

whether they numbered a few dozen or a few thousand. In that way, he was Reese's utter opposite.

"When Victor had his lackeys provoke Sam last night, it wasn't to send a message to *her*," Reese said finally.

Asher grunted. "I thought something was off. If he'd wanted to pressure Samantha, the Academy is a more controlled environment. So what does our fearless leader want with Cassis?"

"Not Cassis either," said Reese. "Me. Victor wants Sam following vampiric protocols, but he can't order a witch to do that without setting off havoc with the council. So he wants me to bully her into it while Victor stands back and waits to be pleasantly surprised by the witch's choice."

"I see." Asher's voice was very, very even.

Reese stopped, turning to Asher and dropping his gaze for a moment in silent apology. He should have told him earlier. Asher was in charge and deserved to know. Reese had stupidly thought he'd had it handled. "I'm sorry."

"Blackmail. Some things never change." Asher's tawny eyes stayed steady on the distant stone towers of the Academy, but Reese had no delusions that his friend was anything but livid. "The presence of a witch, especially one capable of influencing the elements, changes the power dynamic. That's even before we consider what happens when she matures and takes a council seat. It's little wonder that both Bryant and Victor want to break her to their bridle. What are you going to do? Provided you are still considering options beyond running off like a coward."

"I'm not running away," Reese said. "I'm making a strategic retreat. If I stay, the choice is either bend to Victor's blackmail or watch Cassis get hurt over and over again. Take me out of the equation, and the fire dies for lack of oxygen."

"No, it doesn't. Victor will simply find another vampire for the job, and if this *project* is destined to happen, I, for one, would prefer it be handled by someone I trust." Asher sighed, drumming two fingers against his thigh. His voice lowered. "If you aren't ready to spend so much time alone with a witch, I will understand."

The words hit Reese in the gut, and it took all his centuries of training to keep as much from showing in his face. He wasn't afraid of Samantha Devinee, no matter what Ellis's theories suggested or who the witch saw in her strange visions. He *wasn't.*

"If the witch starts practicing vampiric protocols, it will make her appear to side with the vamps," Reese said, turning the tables on Asher instead. "That could start an interspecies war."

Asher shook his head, looking utterly unfazed. "Whether Samantha uses the protocols is a separate conversation—and, frankly, her choice. However, I insist that her choices be educated ones. Last night at Dusk, the girl didn't know Victor's demands were—arguably—appropriate for the environment. All she saw was bullying. It's damn fortunate she didn't contradict Cassis's orders on top of the count's."

Reese felt a noose constricting around his neck. Bloody Asher and his logic.

"I'll talk to her," Reese said, ignoring the way his body tensed in anticipation of Sam's sweet scent. "Explain the rules. Force the knowledge of vampiric protocol down her throat if I have to. Then I'm done. When or whether she uses them is her business. Or yours."

❧

THAT EVENING, Reese leaned against the back wall of the gymnasium, watching his pupil-to-be sink her fists into the canvas punching bag. He'd intended to interrupt her the moment he walked in, but something about the ferocity of the girl's movements gave him pause. Made him hold still in the shadows, unnoticed, while the *thump thump thump* of Samantha's knuckles against the stuffed canvas echoed through the room.

From the way Sam's skin gleamed with sweat under the harsh fluorescent lights, she'd been at the bag for a while. Each time she struck, a faint tremble ran through every inch of her tight body, damp strands of hair escaping her ponytail and sticking to her face and neck. Distantly, Reese noted that her striking form had improved. Ellis was a hell of a trainer.

For a moment, as Reese stood watching Sam, he forgot why it was he came and nearly called out instructions on form. He caught himself in time, but by then, the rawness of the girl's movements drew Reese's attention to her face instead.

Clenched jaw. Flaring nostrils. Eyes bloodshot and glazed over with exhaustion—physical and otherwise. She'd been crying.

Shit.

Reese's hand tightened around the book he'd brought, his stomach clenching as well. He'd come here for a purpose. To inform the witch she'd be learning protocol. Give her a schedule. Maybe scuff her up a little to get her in the right frame of mind. And instead, he found Sam drowning in enough pain to twist air into knots. To make something inside Reese waken with a need to heal it.

Which he certainly wasn't going to do. Was in no fucking way qualified to do. The last thing Reese needed was to get into the witch's business. To let her anywhere near his own.

Sam placed the next blow with great enough force and little enough skill that instead of moving the bag, she knocked herself onto the floor, barely avoiding hitting her head in the process. Scrambling up with the ferocity of a feral cat, the little witch growled in frustration and attacked the bag again, blow after blow after blow—each more likely to hurt herself than the bag. Which, Reese was starting to realize with a heavy, sinking feeling, was probably the point. A way of drowning out one pain with another.

Reese knew that little technique well—he'd done it to himself over and over for centuries.

Before he could reconsider, Reese pushed himself silently off the wall and started toward the girl. A slight tang of sweet copper was seeping into the air now—blood from where Sam skinned her knuckles raw over and over on the rough canvas. Yeah. Reese knew that trick too.

Jaw tight, Reese hooked Sam's leg midstep, tripping the witch neatly onto her back midblow. "What exactly are you punishing yourself over?"

Sam scrambled up to her elbows, glaring at him savagely. Under her tight red racerback, her breasts heaved. And then, she chose to say the one thing that gave Reese no choice but to respond. "Fuck. Off. Sir."

With a short growl, Reese grabbed Sam by the front of her shirt and hauled her to her feet. Ignoring the girl's flailing limbs, he pivoted smoothly and slammed her right into the nearest padded wall. With her feet still dangling above the floor, he stepped in close enough that his breath brushed against her flushed cheeks—and her breasts against his chest, a fact that he pushed way, way down where it belonged.

"Do you want to try that again, cadet?" he demanded, his voice the kind of low, menacing murmur that sent SEAL trainees into blanched silence. The effect on Samantha was similar. The blood left her face, her pupils dilating.

Thank Hades she still had enough wits about her to feel fear.

"I'm sorry for my choice of words, sir." The tepid apology forced itself through Sam's clenched teeth.

"No, I don't think you are," Reese said. "At least not yet."

The flash of Sam's eyes made Reese realize what he'd just said, how closely the demand for a proper apology came to Victor's showdown at Dusk. He opened his mouth, trying and failing to come up with a way to walk that back, but the sinking feeling in his gut told him it was too late.

Sam's lips pulled back into a snarl, the blood that had left her face a moment ago now returning so fast that it made her skin glow. "Do you want me to get on my knees as well? Or should we skip the foreplay and get right to destroying things?"

Reese's head spun from the sudden change in scent. Hers and his. The room's.

How could he simultaneously itch to shake the witch free of that bloody attitude while also wanting to bury himself deep inside all that fiery heat? Samantha radiated a passion that Reese had not felt in centuries, not since Sienna took his wife. Yet here it was, blazing inside her soul. Bright enough to burn them all down.

"You want to pick a fight with me?" Stepping close to her, Reese bared his teeth, his usually quiet heart thumping against his chest, his hand still holding the witch against the wall. "You got it."

With a flex of his hand, Reese launched the witch back to the mat, waiting until she rolled back to her feet and took a swing at him before batting her punch away. "Do you even know what last night was about?" he demanded, deflecting another with insulting ease, as if playing with a kitten. "For that matter, have you any notion of what kneeling means in vampiric terms?"

"Don't know," Sam's chest heaved. "Don't give a fuck."

A growl Reese hadn't realized was brewing inside him escaped his chest, his own slow heartbeat spiking in speed. The witch *should* give a fuck. She damn well owed that little to the rest of them. "So you want to, what, make up rules as you go along?" The words fled from Reese with enough heat to prove just how tenuous his control, his apathy truly was. "You use magic. Dangerous magic you know nothing about and send into the world anyway. Learning our rules is beneath you, but magic—that's just fine. Is that how it works?"

Opening her palms, Sam shoved his chest—for all the good it did. "I never wanted this. The magic, the Academy, vampires, any of it."

"No one cares what you want, witch!" Reese shouted, the words bouncing off the walls as blazing fury spilling into his blood made the room flicker. Hades take him. What the hell was wrong with him? Stepping back, Reese fought down the twin urges to knock Sam into the nearest wall and claim her mouth with his own until neither of them could breathe.

. This needed to end. Now. Whatever had set off the witch's masochistic spiral was her problem to deal with. Reese couldn't go there. Not without losing himself.

Catching Sam's foot as she tried to kick him, Reese knocked her back onto the mat again, this time following her down to press his knee into her solar plexus. The pressure forced the air out of Sam's lungs, her eyes widening as he leveraged the exhale to make himself heavier still. To make her every attempt to draw breath a pain-filled chore.

"Now that I have your attention," Reese said with deliberate slowness, hanging on to the hard-won control of himself he finally reclaimed. "Allow me to enlighten you as to what is going to happen. You are going to learn vampiric protocol. From me. Until I'm bloody satisfied. And then we never have to talk again. Understand?"

Reese lifted his knee, and Sam turned over into a turtle position to regain her breath.

"There's a book by the back wall. *Our Code*. Read it. Love it. Memorize the first four chapters by tomorrow night."

10

Sam

"*W*hy do you have a copy of *Our Code?*" Mika crinkles her nose at the thick volume on my desk. "Are you interested in vampires now?"

"Only as far as I can kill them. No offense." I can still feel the film of rage over my insides at Reese. Vampiric fucking protocols? After the show at Dusk last night, I'll lick dog shit off Victor's shoes if it means saving Cassis's pain, but if Reese thinks it's now open season to squeeze me, he has another thing coming.

I flip the book open onto a random page. *Rule 39: Anticipate your master's desires and strive to fulfill them before he asks. Rule 40: Keep your eyes lowered to the ground. Rule 41: Obedience to your master's orders must be swift and absolute.* Yeah. One day, I'm shoving Reese's fucking *Code* up his ass.

Why is it that the moment men smell weakness—and I know in my gut Reese had marked my tear-streaked face—they suddenly fancy themselves masters of the universe? My hand tightens around the corner of my desk. My own fault for getting caught up in pointless punching when I should have been on alert. Should never have let Reese sneak up on me, watch me trip over my own damn rage.

Mika grins, oblivious to my dark thoughts as she turns back to her laptop. "None taken. But statistically speaking, bowing the wrong way to the right duke rarely leads to death. Actually, I take that all back. I'm sure people got killed over that left and right, but I still have doubts about its effectiveness as an offensive measure. Maybe...consider a sword? It does seem more efficient."

I nudge the book with my pencil, as if I'm poking a bug. "You haven't read it, have you?"

"All the vamps have read it—well, have read the first ten pages, which pretty much cover the basics that get you through most of life. The rest is for the obsessive-compulsive types. And traditionalists. And, probably anyone who wants to get on Victor's good side, since he's the one who wrote it and all."

Did he? That explains so fucking much.

"Back to why you have it," Mika says, spiky black hair swaying as she taps ferociously on her keyboard. Probably reprogramming the showers to spew ice water in the instructors' quarters.

"Lieutenant Reese decided that my evenings would be best spent learning how he and Victor like to have their boots licked." I'm rather proud of the restraint with which I say Victor's name, given how the echoes of his voice still make my stomach churn, how the last whimpering sounds of Cassis's beautiful piano fill my mind. There are so very few things Cassis cares about. And now there is one less.

Because I'm some kind of radioactive thing that gets everyone around me hurt. First Ellis, now Cassis, probably Mika next if I'm not careful. No matter what I do, just by being a witch, I seem to be a one-woman demolition crew. "You really should stay away from me, Mika. Especially in public."

"Been there, talked about that. No." She doesn't even look up from her screen. "What are you gonna do about Reese?"

"Reese thinks I'm easy to break," I say quietly. "I'm going to disabuse him of that notion."

This time Mika does lift her head, blinking at me like a large owl. "Are you insane? Challenge him, and he will kill you, Samantha. Unless you have some magical bomb up your sleeve, you are not besting that male in any fight."

"No, I'm not. Which is why I need to beat him at his own damn game." I jerk my chin toward Mika's computer. "Can you pull up all the Academy regulations for me? Like all the formality rules and everything."

I GO through the following day engrossed in the dual study of Academy protocols—which seem assembled from the various militaries of the world—and the vampiric rules. Each new page of *Our Code* makes my insides twist tighter. It's not just kneeling. It's not just eye contact. It's a dramatic surrender to another will, a sacrifice of all dignity in hopes of winning scraps of a master's good will. That is what Reese wants to do to me.

No. Just, no. I haven't surrendered to anyone else's will since the early years of foster care, and I won't do it now.

Which is going to make these lessons very interesting.

Whenever they happen. After spending the day reading and taking notes and waiting for Reese to crook his finger, I'm drained by the time dinner arrives with no word from the vamp. When nothing happens after dinner either, I start to think that perhaps Reese changed his mind about teaching me manners. Or just forgot.

The possibility of the latter leaves a bitter taste in my mouth—which just pisses me off more. What kind of idiot would want to be remembered by a male she hates?

Shaking off the thought, I celebrate my Reese-free evening by joining Mika in her bed to indulge in bootlegged *Buffy the Vampire Slayer*, killing two episodes before calling it a night. There are definite advantages to having the little hacker in my room, even if it means I get even less sleep than usual. The last thing I need is to be broadcasting my nightmares. Fortunately, Mika wears headphones at night to play some online game and pretends not to notice when I get up in the pit of darkness and take a hot shower.

Changing into pajamas—which, given that I have no money to buy anything, are actually just a clean PT kit—I reluctantly climb into bed, the Russian roulette of nightmares already spinning. Will it be Quinn's attempted rape keeping me company tonight, or blood running down Ellis's back? Or maybe the haunted look in Cassis's eyes last night. So many choices, so little time.

∾

BOOM. Boom. Boom.

I realize that the sound is coming from outside my dream as the door to my chamber clicks open, and a very tall and very male shadow invites himself inside. Scrambling out of bed, I put myself between the imposter and Mika, who squeaks and shoves herself into a corner. My heart pounds, my hand closing around the knife I keep under my pillow nowadays.

"Stand down, witch." Reese's crisp British voice is almost

lazy. Almost. "You have to the count of ten to put on shoes before I drag you outside with or without them."

Before I can draw a lungful of air, Reese closes the distance and grips my wrist, bending it until the knife clatters to the floor. In the room's darkness, he is all silhouette and muscles and an aggressively tangy scent, like a stormy sea. "I'm of a mind to see how well you've learned your assignment." Reese's voice drops so low, I can barely make out the words brushing my ear. "Clearly, not well, if this is your idea of a proper greeting. But we have time to try again. And again. And again. Move."

That last command is no longer quiet, sounding instead like something a military-movie drill sergeant might shout. Or a real drill sergeant, probably. It's the kind of tone that lights a fire beneath every muscle before your brain even catches up.

I'm reminded eerily of the first time Ellis yanked me out of bed for physical training—which seems like decades ago with everything that's happened between then and now.

That's how I end up following Reese into the dim, empty hallway and down the stairs, my breath loud over our hushed footfalls. His back is broad and straight above me, every muscle outlined beneath a tight black T-shirt. My thoughts alternate between silent vows to make this as unsatisfying as possible for the brooding vampire and regrets over staying up late with Buffy. On the bright side, I decide as I step out into the chilly night air, all my preparation yesterday won't be going to waste.

That last thought adds a bit of steel to my spine as we cross to the center of the dark green. The grass swishes wetly over my leather boots, and I suppress a shiver as a bat dips silently overhead. *This isn't your first rodeo with self-aggrandizing men,* I remind myself, *and at least you knew this was coming.*

"I didn't realize learning to grovel was a middle-of-the-night type of activity," I mutter, earning a long sideways glance from Reese.

"I did not realize you preferred learning to grovel with the whole school watching."

Despite myself, I feel a deranged, humorless chuckle race up my throat. Only in this fucked-up place could getting dragged out of bed in the middle of the night to genuflect on the cold ground be considered a favor. Fuck, maybe I really should be thanking the asshole. If I wasn't out here with him, I'd be reliving Quinn's attack. There is nothing Reese can do to me to top that.

Stopping in front of me, Reese puts his hands behind his back and watches, those penetrating blue eyes of his taking in a great deal more than I wish. His messy black hair blows lightly in the night's breeze, the only soft part of him. The opening gambit. I brace myself. Whatever happens next, surrender will not be part of it.

"Well?" he prompts. He wants me to kneel. I know it. I've read the code. He knows I've read the code.

But I read a few other things as well.

I grip Reese's eyes for a moment, then let my gaze slide off them to stare straight ahead into nothingness, my heels together, my hands perfectly extended down the seams of my pants. Attention position, à la the *Talonswood Reform Academy Manual*.

"Wrong book, witch," says Reese. "Wrong battle plan."

I say nothing. I know what's coming. So long as Reese is prepared to watch me throw up—because that is going to happen despite Ellis's best efforts to build my stamina—we are on the same page. On the other end of the green, the sand pit is looking more like a battleground than a torment chamber.

"This would be a good time to apologize for not doing

what you know I'm asking for." Reese's voice is gravelly, the reined-in threat sending a shiver along my skin.

"Sir. This cadet apologizes, sir."

Reese actually huffs a small laugh. "Are you aware that I have a bit of experience with the human military?" he asks nonchalantly. "American SEAL team, the SAS for the Brits. Delta Force."

"Sir, this cadet isn't sure which armed forces you served in, sir." A perfectly appropriate response. And utterly not what Lieutenant Reese wants to hear.

Too bad for him he can't tell me to cut it out, not without overtly contradicting the Academy's regulations. Vampiric high protocol is a preference. A style. Parties can choose to indulge in it, but it isn't the official language of Talonswood. This is.

I'm smart enough to hide an ironic smile as Reese watches me in silence, blue eyes unreadable, tapping a finger against his thigh.

"The problem for you, Devinee," he says after a moment, "is that the little tricks you think you've invented, I've long since forgotten. But I'll tell you what. Let's play this evening out by your rules."

For the first time, a shadow of doubt brushes my chest.

"Ca—DET." Reese suddenly sounds nothing like himself, the quiet brooding transformed into a deep full-chested bellow as his eyes become cold and hard, his expressive mouth hardening into a granite line. His posture shifts too, his shoulders rolling back into a military rigidity that makes him look separate from the human race—and not just because he's a vampire. "On the ground. Plank."

Here we go. Snatching a final fortifying breath, I drop into pushup position. Arms stretched. Elbows locked. Head up, eyes locked forward.

Reese's boot presses into my side, knocking me over into the dirt. "I said plank. Not sag like a dirty laundry sheet."

I get back up, my muscles tight.

Reese knocks me down.

Again. And again. And again. The anger in my veins rises slowly. I have the position right. The asshole knows it.

"Holy bloody hell, has the notion of a straight line escaped you completely, Devinee? Or are you rebelling against geometry?" Reese snarls, dropping down to the ground beside me, my arms now trembling from the strain. "You have a hundred push-ups to deliver, and so far, you are going *backward*. I don't think I've seen such a damn feat before."

He knocks me over. "Maybe some good will come from this yet. I want you to remember this moment the next time you so much as think about reaching for magic. If you can't do this, you've got no business near witchcraft."

I get back up. Fire fills my muscles, the grains of dirt starting to work themselves into my clothes and skin and eyes. *Why the fuck am I even playing this game?* The thought comes unbidden as I blink sweat away. *Why not drop to my knees, bow my head, and count the seconds until this humiliation is over?*

Because I'm better than that. Because I didn't spend twenty years fending for myself, following my own code, only to give up now. I clench my jaw, desperately trying to believe my own pep talk. Because this will end. Because no man is going to break me.

"Let's see if you've grown any more capable of running in a straight line than you are doing a push-up." Reese's cold voice slashes across me.

We're both keenly aware I can run about as well as I can pee standing up.

For a second, I'm actually tempted to tell him as much, but I manage to keep my mouth shut as I stumble after him on a punishing run. We do the three-mile loop through the forest trails as the first grayness of dawn just breaks through the trees. The loop that's so easy for everyone else and leaves me with a stitch in my side and the world shimmering at the edges. I'd be relieved when Reese's steps finally slow, but he's brought me to the damn sand I had a feeling we'd be visiting.

"I said *plank*, Devinee." Reese hollers into my face, as I shake and drop, his own strong pale features shadowed in the near dark. My arms trying and failing to find purchase. "Are you incompetent or just fucking stupid?"

"Sir. This cadet is fucking stupid, s—" I have a mouth full of sand before I finish the words, Reese's boot hitting what's now a growing bruise on my side. My blood simmers, anger overpowering the chill of the night. There is no point to this. No amount of effort that will ever create the mystery perfect plank Reese is after because the damn thing doesn't fucking exist.

The bastard is making it up as he goes along.

Again. And again. Pulling me out of the sand pit for a new flavor of misery—a run through an obstacle course until my legs and arms are shaking, a wall climb that has me falling onto my back, a log lift that leaves my abs too weak to contract —and then dragging me right back to the same spot. The same sand. The same game, over and over.

Funny how understanding the game doesn't take away its power.

"Lock it up," Reese snaps.

I clamber to my feet, the sand inside my shirt and pants and bra rubbing my skin raw. My arms ache, shaking even as I strike the ordered attention, my heels and calves and thighs pressing together, my thumbs tracing the trouser seams. My eyes straight ahead. Bracing. Waiting. Shivering.

"Am I disrupting your night? Have you something better to

be doing just now?" Reese's face is so close to mine that I feel the light heat his vampiric body produces, smell his tangy cologne of fresh ocean breeze, a bit of mint and male musk. Feel and smell, but don't see, not with the male standing just off center from my straight-ahead gaze. "That wasn't rhetorical, witch." Reese's breath brushes my cheek, his words dripping with contempt. "Answer me."

"Sir. No, sir." At least that much is truthful. Fuck it. Maybe I'm kidding myself. Maybe I'm not here to make a point or stand up for pride. Maybe I'm out here pissing off Reese because it's better than being alone with my nightmares. Maybe, just fucking maybe, I'm here because I deserve every last bit of this. "Nowhere better, sir."

I'm exactly where I should be.

11

Reese

*R*eese froze, the flash of pain coming off Sam hitting him in the gut with soul-wrenching precision. What the bloody hell was he doing peeling away the witch's defenses when he'd promised himself to stay away? To not get involved in whatever it was that haunted her. And yet here they were, her trembling from a great deal more than cold and fatigue and him in too deep to stop now.

It was the second time in as many days that the girl baited him into a punishing routine, except this time, he had no one to blame but himself. She'd challenged him, and, like a juvenile unable to back away, Reese reacted. How many centuries had it been since someone could get under his skin so swiftly?

Well, now the bill had come due. With her shields cracking under Reese's merciless pressure, Sam now wore that look he'd seen on more soldiers' faces than he cared to count—an overwhelmed, pain-racked dread that destroyed souls if left to fester. That protective feeling rose up inside Reese again, the one longing to heal her pain. And, unlike in the training room, backing away like a coward was no longer an option, not when he'd been the one to slice open the wound.

All right. Tension raced through Reese's spine, his heart quickening as he mentally sprinted through her past weeks. Bernadette's betrayal. Imprisonment. Quinn's near rape. His death. Ellis. The piano. Any one of those traumas would be enough to drive someone into a hell, but from Sam's heaving chest and glazed eyes, from the way she was a glutton for punishment, she wasn't just reliving them. She was blaming herself for every damn one.

Bloody hell.

Sam swallowed expectantly, reminding him that it was time to get on with it. To break her enough to allow for the emotional readjustment he owed her. And try like hell not to shatter himself in the process.

Reese's throat tightened. He was making the witch's wounds his problem, wrapping himself so deeply inside her pain that he might not crawl out. It was a cliff he'd been approaching for days—and now he was about to sprint headlong over it.

Right. Might as well commit to the fall. Bracing himself, Reese tried to recall what insult track he'd been on when the truth punched him in the gut. Yes, whether she thought she was in the right place. Shifting his weight, Reese reached back for the routine that came too easily after centuries of an all-you-can-march buffet of military training.

"Well, thank the bloody heavens you think so, because I would hate to impose," Reese shouted across the witch's stricken face. Familiar insults that were no longer easy to throw. "Or to let pass this opportunity to learn from your great wisdom, Devinee. So much smarter than the rest of us. A witch who knows everything. Who owes no respect, no apologies, no consideration to anyone in Talonswood. Fuck, maybe we have it all wrong. Maybe it's the rest of us who owe *you*. Is that what you think, Devinee? Do the rest of us owe you something?"

Sam flinched, color gripping her neck and face, anger that she still could somehow summon spilling into her scent. "No one owes me anything, sir." She spat the words at him, glaring into his eyes. "I have been crystal clear on that much for a long time."

"Oh, you're looking at me now? What is it? Too good to lower your gaze, too undisciplined to keep it raised. A bit of a mixed message, don't you think?" Reese twisted his mouth into a cruel snarl and loomed over her, his power pushing in like a physical force. "Was that what happened with Quinn too? Did you mix up your messages? Let the poor bugger think you *wanted* to be fucked and then changed your mind?"

Samantha's hazel eyes flashed with fury, and Reese was careful to grab her wrist before the fist she was making could take flight. Gray light paled into lavender around them, the sand pit and Samantha and the surrounding training yard climbing out of the shadows. Not that he needed the light to see every inch of the girl. She was beautiful in her fury.

Samantha swallowed. Opened her mouth.

Reese shoved her back down to the ground, ensuring she had a mouthful of sand to spit out before she could consider talking. "Push."

She couldn't. But she tried anyway. Her slender arms tight and cramping, her body shaking so badly that bits of sand flew off her blue PT kit into the air. The scent of her fury filled Reese's lungs. But he couldn't back off. Couldn't lose focus Not now. Grabbing a bucket of water he'd prepared, he doused the girl with icy liquid and stood back as she screamed.

"Push," Reese yelled over her. "I'd have thought a single-word command was short enough even for you to understand." He dropped until his face was inches from Sam's, her scent making his head swim. "But maybe I've figured you out. You *don't* understand. You grab and run. You break everything you touch. But that's why you're here in Talonswood, isn't it? Bryant dangled money in front of you, and you ran like a greedy streetwalker. *Push.*"

Sam's breath hitched.

"Hades take me. One bloody pushup is taking half the night. I'm immortal, and even I don't have the patience for the next ninety-nine."

"Ten." Sam's jaw clenched, her teeth grinding so hard that Reese could hear them. "I've done ten."

"You've done zero. That was one charity push-up that I counted." Reese loomed over her, moving as she did. Never letting up. "A greedy little witch, but a piss-poor one. Good thing you've managed to get others to do your dirty work. Ellis. Remember him? He's the one who bled for you. Killed for you. All because— " Reese's words caught in his throat as Sam's scent shifted like a breaking storm.

Thank Hades she was finally cracking, because Reese didn't think he could keep this up for much longer.

"You break everything you touch," Reese dropped his voice as Sam's eyes closed, her body dropping to the sand. "Ellis. Cassis. Asher too. Do you know how long he worked to get this academy organized before you lured Victor here?"

A sob escaped her chest.

He could barely continue now, her scent so saturated with pain that his throat closed, his hands itching to comfort her. It'd never been like this before. Fuck, he'd never wanted it to be over this badly before.

"Do you?" Reese shouted mercilessly into her ear. "Do

you?" Over and over, watching as she flinched from the verbal blows. Feeling them land just as heavily on his own chest.

"Yes," Sam cried, her words filling the empty training yard, ripping Reese's soul to shreds. Tears slid down her face, which she no longer tried to cover. Her whole body trembling before him. "It's all my fault," she sobbed into the ground. "I'm sorry. I am so, so sorry."

Hades take him.

Reese felt as though his insides were pooled beside her in the sand. It took all his self-control to stay still. To give Samantha the time she needed. But when she raised her face to him, her eyes begging him to inflict whatever pain could drown out the one tearing her apart from within, his restraint broke.

He hadn't been prepared for this part. Hadn't trained for it. He was far, far out at sea, drifting in her scent, her brimming hazel eyes, her pain, willing to do anything to make them stop. Just as he'd begged Sienna to make his wife's pain stop. He couldn't bear it.

Taking her tear-streaked face into his hands, Reese lifted it gently until he could catch her large eyes and prayed to whatever deity was listening that Sam was ready to believe him now. "It isn't your fault, Samantha. None of it. You no more could have stopped what happened than you could have done a push-up I'd have said was acceptable. The rules were rigged."

"But you said—"

"I said what you were telling yourself. But—with the exception of the bit about you not being ready to manipulate magic—none of it is true. None. And you need to know that." Reese exhaled, pushing a lock of Sam's sweat-soaked hair behind her ear. Hades, she was beautiful. And hurting so much that Reese wanted to sink his fist into the nearest brick wall for having done that to her. "There is a great deal at stake, Samantha, and none of it will be built on a foundation of lies. Ones to yourself included. Quinn was a filthy bastard who deserved what he got. And Ellis would step in again in a heartbeat to save you. As would I. Or Asher. Or Cassis. You are responsible for none of it, Sam. You don't hold the reins in this world, and you're going to have to be okay with that. You're not always in control."

He watched her face, could practically read the thoughts there—her brief, hard life in the mortal world, all the many decisions she'd had to make for herself there. Never trusting anyone or taking a handout. That would all have to change—now.

"You'll need help navigating this world, Sam. My help. Others'. Can you accept it?""

She blinked. Drew a gasping breath. Stared at Reese as if she feared to put too much stock in his words lest they be yanked back. But at least she wasn't hiding now. It was a start.

Sliding his hands under her, Reese cradled her against his chest. So small and light. So filled with passion that she burned even herself. That she allowed him to carry her, especially after what he'd done, was a gift Reese knew better than to underestimate. A gift that shook him to his very core, raising questions he wasn't willing to even begin answering.

As Sam pressed her head into his shoulder, her body still trembling but not hiding from him, he made quick calculations. He needed to get her warm, and she needed not to have an audience. Not the cadets' barracks then. The infirmary? Too sterile. And possibly too intimidating given her last visit there. His room, then. Pulling a phone from his pocket, Reese sent Asher a quick text message to make himself scarce and headed inside.

12

Sam

It isn't your fault, Samantha. None of it.

I tremble against Reese's hard chest, my body spent, my emotions leaking onto my cheeks. When I draw a shaking breath, the male's arms tighten around me. Protective. Secure. Confident.

A male I barely knew when I went to sleep last night, who now carries me as if I weigh nothing. His skin is cool, and his scent washes over me, bathing my senses in minty, tangy sea air.

Reese heads into the instructor's wing and inside a large, plain suite I assume must be his—two leather armchairs and a couch, a soft blue rug, bare fireplace, and flat-screen TV. And, through the two open doors on either end, beds.

My heart quickens, and Reese stops, his blue gaze brushing me with too much understanding.

"You've nothing more to fear from me, Samantha. Not today."

"I like the qualifier."

Snorting softly, Reese walks us into the bathroom, which is larger than some of the rooms I've shared in foster care. When he sets me down on top of the large marble vanity, his hand lingering on my shoulder for a moment, I realize I need the wall just to keep myself from falling.

I immediately feel the loss of Reese's presence when he steps away, though the sound of running water filling the room a moment later explains what he's doing. Warm steam escapes from the frosted shower door, moistening the air. Returning to me, Reese bends to pull off my boots and socks, his thick, dark hair shining in the low light.

"I can do it my—"

Reese snaps me a look, cutting me off midword. "What did I say?"

I can't help the small smile that creeps onto my face, remembering his words. *Can you accept help?*

"And it's not because you are a weak person, Samantha, but because I wore out your body. This is my doing. Do you understand?"

I nod.

Still, he bends before me, his face level with mine. "It's crucial that you do. You'll need to hold your own in this world, just like you used to in yours, but you'll need to learn to be part of it too. When we do get around to teaching you vampire protocol, you'll understand that kneeling and bowing are symbols. Like shaking hands and saluting, they only negotiate power if you let them. But sometimes, with the right person, you should let them. You can give up control while still holding on to yourself. Am I clear?"

Reese waits, pinning me in place with his eyes.

Finally, I nod, and he picks me up again, carrying me under the stream of hot water, clothing and all. It's a heady, strange experience giving up control, but I'm too exhausted to care. For several long heartbeats, we just stand there, my head resting on his shoulder, getting wet and warm under the pounding shower spray. Comfortable. Which would be a good thing if that damn comfort didn't also let my thoughts come racing back.

Squirming out of his arms, I let my feet settle on the tile floor, the calmness of the past moments fading. "No matter what you say, no matter what I meant to do—I still got everyone hurt, Reese." I take a step back from him. "You know it. I know it. Why—"

"Stop." Reese's sharp British order echoes off the wet walls, and my mouth shuts without consulting my brain.

I'm tired. Of fighting. Of feeling. Of being wrong all the fucking time. And something about the solid confidence of Reese's order feels like an anchor I can hold on to.

"Thank Hades." Reese rubs his face, wiping away water that streams along his strong cheekbones. His black T-shirt is plastered to his torso, his biceps straining the sleeves. This close to him, I have to crane my neck back to meet his eyes, to trace the sculpted angles of his face. "What am I going to do with you, Samantha?" He holds out his hand as I open my mouth to reply. "Rhetorical question."

Reaching out, he takes my chin in his hand, his brilliant blue gaze piercing into me. "I've worked you enough for one night, but that mind of yours won't let you rest, will it? All right. Then we are going to do something else." Reese steps even closer, crowding my space, his hold on my jaw tightening. His voice is not unkind when he speaks again, but it's not yielding either. "I'm going to take the reins for a while, the way my vampiric instincts pull me to do. I may not be able to compel you, but you are going to let me, Samantha. Willingly. Silently."

My eyes widen, and Reese shakes his head quickly. "I've no intention of taking you sexually. I've never forced a woman in my life, and I'm not about to start with a witch." The words should be hurtful, but they aren't. "But I will take charge."

I swallow at the strange rush of heat Reese's words send through my core, despite the glare I give him.

Before I realize what's happening, Reese pulls my shirt over my head with the practiced ease of a male who's been removing women's clothing for many centuries. The shock of hot water against my sandy skin mixes with the headiness of being shirtless before Reese. I clasp my hands across my chest protectively.

Reese shakes his head in warning, and my arms drop away, my breath stopping as my bra follows the same way as my shirt.

Reese's blue eyes brush my body slowly, then return to my face, nothing betraying his thoughts but a tiny tic in his jaw. "You've nothing to hide, Sam. I've seen you naked before."

Right. The hosing down on the first day. I cringe, but my knees soften. Being naked in front of Reese makes me feel vulnerable, but not lewd. Which is somehow hot as hell.

He reaches over my shoulder, brushing my skin with one thickly muscled arm, and his cool skin against the hot water makes me jump. Fuck. He could break my neck with those arms and not even realize something was in his way. In the back of my mind, Cassis's warning purrs over my thoughts.

Don't mistake my control for safety. Not with me, not with any of my kind. Do you understand?

My heart quickens, the shower stall tightening around me. And yet, somehow, the shot of fear flushing my veins only feeds my arousal.

Reese's arm pulls back, blue gel pooling in his large palm, the shampoo's smell already filling the humid air. Ignoring the tension in my body, Reese spreads the gel over my hair, strong fingers massaging it into my scalp while the water running down my body clears away the sand.

My breath rushes out of me in quick bursts. My breasts feel achy, full, just from seeing the ridges of Reese's body revealed beneath wet clothes, and yet I can't tell apart the arousal from the fear. And the humiliation that I should feel but somehow don't. I know I should be doing something. Covering myself up or, at the very least, shampooing my own hair. In fact, I should—

"Stop thinking," Reese orders. "There is nothing that you can do that's wrong, because I am telling you exactly what to do. In fact, turn around and put your hands on the wall. Palms flat."

Seriously?

He raises one dark brow. "If I smack your wet ass right now," he whispers softly into my ear, "it will sting very much."

Heat rushes from my cheeks right to my sex, which is wet from more than shower water. I unclench my fingers from my training pants and press them against the cool tile. For a moment, nothing happens, and a shiver runs over my skin. Then I feel Reese's callused hands brush over my aching muscles, gently washing away the dirt and sweat.

No one does this for me, much less a hot navy SEAL vampire with a British accent and a way of sending electrical pulses from my breasts to my clit just by ordering me to turn around and shut up. Holy crap. A shudder I can't control escapes me as Reese's hands lift my aching breasts and brush away the grains of sand that managed to get there too.

I don't remember anyone ever helping me bathe before, even as a small child. Most foster moms tried to touch me as little as possible, as if being an orphan was somehow infectious. And then I learned that not being touched at all was better than the alternative.

Until now. I'm just beginning to relax under Reese's touch when his hands drop to the top of my pants.

"Don't even think about moving," Reese says hoarsely into my ear. I can barely force the air back into my constricting lungs, my sex pulsing with ever brush of Reese's words over my skin. "Or speaking."

I'm still wondering whether vampires can smell arousal when my sweatpants drop to the tile floor with a wet slap. Reese has me bare, and all coherent thoughts simply disappear. Something brushes my ass—the wet cotton of Reese's pants as he steps closer to me. His hands slide competently along my thighs, the scrape of his calluses along my skin making my core sing like the most clear fucking soprano I've ever heard.

But he never touches me. Not *that* way. And I don't know whether I love or hate him for keeping his word.

13

Reese

*R*eese never meant to watch Samantha sleep.

He'd meant merely to help get the sand off her, to take the reins long enough to give her the respite she needed. She deserved. To prove that she did not always have to be the only one looking out for herself. Yet the whole of his self-control had been strained to the limit at the sight of her delicious body, small and leanly muscled, water running down her smooth skin, beading in the fine hairs at the nape of her neck, the tiny dimple over her ass.

And then he'd meant to make himself scarce—give her his bed to sleep away what was left of the morning. It wasn't as if he actually used it more than a few hours every month or so. With some luck, Sam might sleep well into the morning—after what he'd put her through, she'd need it.

It hadn't gone as planned. And that was the bloody understatement of the century.

Reese had started the night fully expecting to force

protocols on the witch. Then she'd mouthed off enough for a change of plans, Reese's military training taking over to put a young recruit into place. And then...then the world shifted around him.

He hadn't meant to care. Certainly hadn't meant to take control of her the way a vampire did for a mate in need. But she'd given him her trust, and the gift of that was too precious to resist, to treat with anything but the utmost reverence it deserved.

Even then, it was supposed to have been all about her. Educating. Correcting. Protecting. But then, somewhere along the way, it became about him too.

In the shower in the wee hours of this morning, when he smelled Samantha's arousal, his world had shaken hard enough that he'd had to brace himself against the tiled wall. Arousal meant, if not complete trust, an openness to it. After he'd shoved her through hell, slicing open the limits of her physical and emotional endurance to expose the wounds deep inside— she was still willing to trust him. Allowed her body to want him.

It had taken all of Reese's strength not to give her body what it wanted and sink his fingers deep into that warmth, to drop his own pants and take her hard against the tile wall. She would have let him. And she would have hated him afterward, undoing all the work he'd done to get her to open up.

She had been asleep nearly as soon as her head touched the pillow. And then semiawake just as quickly moments later, gasping. Screaming in the throes of a nightmare. When Reese heard her scream Quinn's name in utter terror, he had to leave the room to put his fist through a wall. He'd have to explain that hole to Asher.

Something was happening to him. A protective instinct coiling everything inside him into a tight, uncomfortable knot, redirecting all his senses toward a new north—toward her. And it terrified him.

He'd meant to wake her when he returned to the room, but for some reason known to Hades alone, her muscles relaxed when he sat beside her. Her breathing eased as he slid his hand along her soft, trembling back.

That Samantha's nightmares eased with his presence only tightened that knot further, made it rise into his throat with the strength of a vise. He hadn't felt this way in four hundred years, and he'd planned to never again.

Reese had tried to leave two more times, but each time, her terrors started again, with only the names she screamed changing. The girl was reliving things she should never have dealt with. And, if Reese heard right, things that had not happened to *her* at all.

It was five in the morning when she first shouted Sienna's name, thrashing against the sheets as if she'd been strapped down. A scene all too familiar from Reese's own—mercifully rare—dreams. A scene that happened centuries before Samantha was born.

What the bloody hell?

Rolling up his sleeve, Reese ran the tip of his finger over the five-pointed star Sienna's ministrations had left on his forearm. The same one that was on Sam's palm, finally splayed open as her breath slowed with his touch.

So he hadn't left. Sleep was not something that came often to him, but after he wrapped Sam in his arms and felt her sleeping body ease against his, he'd actually settled into the first slumber he'd had in months.

It was already past seven when he blinked awake, the noises outside his bedchamber announcing that Asher had company. Buttoning his sleeve, Reese closed the door behind him as he walked into the common room and cut his gaze over his visitors. The sight of Ellis made him tense.

She is likely your mate too, Ellis had told him.

Reese wanted to kill him for that.

Ellis's nostrils flared delicately, a sly grin coming over his pain-filled features. "I smell Samantha Devinee all over you, Reesand," he said, cocking his head.

"She's sleeping in the other room," Reese answered curtly. There was little point in denying it. "I smell fever all over you, Ellis."

Ellis's grin faltered for a moment before returning. "Then you and Asher can commiserate about your oversensitive noses. Excuse me."

Asher blocked Ellis's path, crossing his arms over his chest. It was still strange to watch Asher give Ellis orders, much less have the fae warrior accept them. But this was more than an instructor and cadet—Asher was standing before his half brother because he was truly worried. And while Reese would be more than happy to see Ellis disappear, Asher wouldn't be.

And neither would Sam. Hades take him.

"Take off your shirt," Reese said, rolling up his sleeves and heading over to the kitchenette sink to wash his hands.

"Why, Reesand, I didn't know I was your type. Won't you buy me a drink first?"

Reese didn't bother answering the provocation, but the fact that Ellis was complying with no more than a cursory fuck-off made him as worried as Asher seemed to be. Then he turned around and swore.

The male's wounds weren't healing. In fact, red streaks now spread onto previously untouched flesh, like a network of angry welts. It was a miracle the male could move without screaming in pain—but then, Ellis was good at hiding such things.

"Why the fucking hell am I only seeing this now?" Reese snapped, keeping his voice low to keep from waking Sam. "If you wanted to kill yourself, Ellis, I would have happily done the deed for you. So want to tell me what stupidity had you curled up in your quarters like a cub with a tucked tail?" Reese palpated along the injured flesh as he spoke, pressing just hard enough at the end of his statement to hear Ellis hiss in pain instead of giving him a smartass reply.

"Iron poisoning," Asher said, his face grim. The male blamed himself. Of course he did. "All because I—"

"All because I killed Victor's pet crony." Ellis snatched his shirt from the table, pulling it back on with a wince. "The point is that this reaction should never have happened. Not from a few lashes."

"A hundred," said Asher.

"We're all proud you can count that high, but there's no need to keep showing off," said Ellis.

"I should have checked the whip, seen if anyone tampered with it." Asher rubbed his face.

"Tampered with a bit of leather and iron that Victor handed you directly?" Reese demanded. "What would you have looked for, pray tell? A hazmat sticker?" Reese turned toward Ellis, who, for once, was acting like the more rational of the brothers. "We don't know that's the root cause. Maybe there was something on the whip. Maybe it's your unlucky streak. Maybe the witch makes you more vulnerable than you thought. Right now, Ellis, it no longer matters. You need to go back to Talon. Your magic will be stronger there, and there are healers who can deal with it in a way I can't."

"No." Ellis's face hardened. "I'm not leaving Devinee here."

"You aren't going to do her any good being dead either." Reese spread his shoulders. Ellis wasn't easy to loom over, but it helped that he was in pain, and Reese wasn't above using any means at hand to get his point across. "Stupidity is more deadly than iron."

"I never knew you cared." Ellis swallowed, his chin lifting in that way that said arguing would be futile. "If you so badly want me to live, then come up with a better idea than using the witch or getting me a ticket to magic land."

Right. Throwing one last look at the closed door where Sam was sleeping, Reese felt his poor judgment taking over. Fine. Fine, he would do something—though waiting until Ellis went unconscious and then throwing him bodily through the gateway still seemed the better option.

Tightening his jaw, Reese pointed to Asher. "You. Infirmary. Now."

Ellis raised a finger. "Point of clarification—"

"Shut the fuck up, you arse," Reese snapped at Ellis before twisting to Asher. "You are donating blood. Let's go."

14

Sam

Sitting beside Mika in the library, I try to follow the equations she's writing in a notebook, her voice way too excited to be explaining exactly how two numbers fit together. They make no more sense to me now than they did in calc, when the vamp teaching the class covered a whole chalkboard with examples.

Or maybe the problem is that no matter what I do, I can't escape my own thoughts of Reese. The way he cracked through every one of my shields. Pushed me to misery and beyond. The way he touched me afterward. The way he didn't touch me.

The Mahogany Hall Library is the perfect place to put that steamy shower out of my mind, with its whispering silence and towering shelves of knowledge. It's the research center for the entire island, not just the reform school, so it's proportionally epic—we sit huddled together at a round table on the ground floor, six levels towering above us in the vaulted space. Slants of light shoot down from a massive octagonal skylight at the very top, catching dust motes on their way down.

"…and then aliens landed."

I nod along before shaking myself like a dog. "Wait. What?"

Mika snorts delicately, flipping a strand of black hair out of her eyes. "Just checking how much you're listening. By my count, you've written down notes on aliens, raccoons, and cockroaches at least three times in the last fifteen minutes, so…"

Looking down at my notebook, I see that Mika is right. "You're no better when it comes to art history," I say, reaching for the old strategy that got me through foster care—a strong defense is a good offense.

Mika snorts again, pointed canines flashing with a little grin. It's school hours, so she's in the same uniform I am—the only girl at the Academy who manages to make the blue skirt look modestly long. But somehow, she's found a way to make it her own—geometric neon-pink stud earrings peeking out of her spiky black bob, oversized old-man glasses that she says are for "blocking blue light," a tiny round pin on one of her shirt cuffs that says, "Machine shop."

The girl and I turn out to have remarkably convenient interests when it comes to schoolwork—in that they're the direct opposite of each other. If we could divide up the exams so she covers all the sciences and I take the creatives, we'd be golden.

Mika shifts in her seat, her features twisting sourly as she focuses on something over my shoulder. "Don't look now, but His Highness Count Victor just graced the Mahogany Hall Library with his immortal presence." She mimes sticking her index finger down her throat.

My shoulders tighten. "The rest of the demivamps are falling over themselves for a chance to lick his shoes."

"I'm smarter than them." Mika chews on her pen. She isn't smart—she's fucking brilliant—but she's also the kind of genius who sometimes has little common sense to speak of. There is literally nothing to gain and lots to lose for a demivamp who refuses to play along.

Shit. I sound like Reese.

"Incoming," Mika murmurs.

Turning around, I see that Victor isn't just taking a stroll down the hardwood library aisle, but has set sights directly for the table where Mika and I huddle. The demifae students rise to their feet, saluting the dean as he passes. Most of the demivamps choose to drop to their knees instead, or at least those seated drop their gazes to the floor. It looks like a wave at a baseball game.

Mika and I get to our feet as Victor stops beside our table, and I lower my gaze to the floor. Not as a way of groveling, but because Reese is right, it's only surrender if that's the meaning I give to the gesture. Otherwise, it's just an arbitrary set of rules in a game of etiquette.

"At ease." Victor's voice echoes through the cavernous hall as he waves his hand in the air, sending the rest of the library back to their studies. Without looking away from the floor, I slide back into my books as well, hoping the vamp is going to move on. But I can feel his gaze on me. Cool, like little snowflakes dancing along my skin.

"I'm pleased to see you've located your manners, Ms. Devinee," Victor says, his voice slow and cultured. He's wearing his signature outfit, a fine silk suit, this one with tiny gray pinstripes and a single red rose pinned to his chest pocket. "It would have been such a shame if you'd lost them for good and all. Perhaps now we can start over from a place of mutual respect."

I swallow against the bile gagging my throat. Last time Victor felt insulted, one of my friends got hurt. Keeping Mika safe is more important than fighting centuries of lore. Arbitrary rules can't make me inferior without my consent. "Yes, Your Excellence."

He smiles. "I wish to discuss a few things with you, if this is a convenient time."

"Of course." I'm smart enough by now to know that only a masochistic idiot would find a meeting with the Talonswood Reform dean *inconvenient*. "I am at your disposal."

"Lovely." Victor gestures toward the huge spiral staircase that is the crown jewel of the Mahogany, winding through the center of the hall.

With the vampire in the lead, we climb the steps though all six floors, stopping by the huge bay window at the very top. Outside, the pristine, tree-filled green sprawls below a cloudless blue sky, surrounded by tall gothic buildings with delicate ivy climbing up their walls.

"The librarians tell me you've been inquiring after texts on witchcraft," Victor says as we both look out the window.

I tense. I *did* inquire, was hoping to learn more about who I am without bringing the world down on top of my head at random intervals. Neither the librarians nor catalog searches led me anywhere, though. "I did not realize researching witchcraft was against the rules, sir."

"Of course it isn't, my dear." Victor places his hands behind his back in a courtly manner, the motion looking utterly natural on him. His pointed features are relaxed, his dark eyes eagle sharp. "But some of my colleagues have thought to remove such literature from student reach. They feel it is a threat to have witches run amok with power, you see."

"They?" I also put my hands behind my back, gripping one of my wrists. "That's a very specific choice of pronoun, sir."

Victor chuckles. "Ah. That fire in you. There it always is, burning so very bright. Very few creatures would permit themselves to be quite so direct with me, and yet I find you refreshing, Samantha. All right, let us both be more direct. Most of the texts on witchcraft were destroyed right along with the witches themselves. Mind you, there were few texts to begin with since the witch covens had oral traditions. The fae-vampire wars brought a dark time for creatures, with a great deal of animosity toward the witches specifically.

"Ultimately, the fae made an effort to take all the remaining books on witchcraft into Talon, both to secure their position in the mortal realm and to see whether they could assimilate any of the witches' knowledge. In short, vampires got the science and the fae took the magic."

"Can they?" I ask. "Can the fae use any witchcraft from the texts they took?"

Excitement simmers in my veins as Victor opens a door I've been pounding on for weeks, but I do my best to keep it from my face. I'm not an idiot. I know that anything he says to me could be a bald-faced lie—but when it comes to magic, I'm just desperate enough to listen anyway.

"I've not been to Talon in some time, but if anything was developed, it would be there. As I've no doubt you learned by now, the mortal world inhibits organic magic for all but the witches. Except for certain innate powers, such as shifting and compulsion."

I consider Victor's words carefully. I've learned to listen for the words people choose to use. The words they choose to omit.

"You said 'made an effort,' sir. Does that mean they didn't manage to take all the library's magic books to Talon?"

Victor gestures to the stacks. "There are no books remaining here, yes. Asher banished them."

Asher. My chest tightens, and I see a corner of Victor's mouth twitch up. He could just be playing me—I'm sure nothing would make him happier than to sour my feelings for the fae. But unfortunately, I don't have any evidence to say he's wrong. Besides Ellis showing me the opening spell when both our lives depended on it, no one has tried to teach me anything about witch magic—though both vamp and fae students receive instruction in developing and controlling whatever powers they have.

If anything, Reese seems to think witchcraft is a dirty, dangerous little habit that needs to be disciplined out of me.

Keeping my face schooled, I wait for Victor to continue. Because I have a feeling he's about to get to the crux of this conversation.

"Fortunately, Mahogany Hall is not the only source of information on the island. One of the advantages of a long life span is that some of us have developed personal libraries. Mine happens to have a volume that may help us unlock your full potential, Samantha. The question is, are you ready?"

I swallow. He has a game. I know he does. The problem is, the apple he holds out toward me is too tempting to resist. Do I want to know what I can do to not be afraid of my own power? To stand toe to toe with Reese and Ellis and the damn cadets with something other than my fists for defense?

My pulse patters in my throat, the thrill of discovery zipping through my veins.

Whatever his plans, I have my own—I can get out of this

project exactly what I want, and I'll keep my eyes wide open the whole time.

"Yes, I am."

"One thing, Samantha. I would not like this to create any conflict within the school, especially given Commander Asher's decision to remove all witchcraft texts from the Mahogany. Please ensure your discretion when practicing." Victor's eyes meet mine, his dark pupils widening in a way that freezes me in place, a soft, warm gauze slipping over my mind. It feels nice. "I'd like no one to know you are working with me. Do you understand?"

"I do," I hear myself say.

15

Sam

The next few days pass in a whirlwind, my thoughts spinning too quickly for me to catch up with. I'm too excited to worry about my next "manners lesson" with Reese, or the fact that Ellis is still ignoring me in the dining hall. On Friday afternoon, Victor sends me instructions to meet him at the chemistry lab that evening—which instantly makes the day drag on as if dialed down to slow motion.

Deep in the science wing of the academic building, the chem lab is used only by third- and fourth-year cadets who've earned the right to select electives. At long last, I wind there through tall white-walled hallways utterly deserted for the night, only single wall sconces every ten feet or so lighting the way.

Walking in to find Victor wearing a white lab coat, titrating something in a beaker, I have the ironic image of a vamp choosing a Halloween costume—but manage to tamp down the sudden manic burst of laughter just in time.

"Eye of newt, toe of frog?" I say under my breath.

Victor looks up, closing the notebook in front of him. "Not at all. This actually has nothing to do with you whatsoever, Samantha. I simply was using the opportunity of an available lab to indulge in a bit of my own research. You will find that with our life span, many vampires take comfort in science. Now, then." Victor focuses all his attention on me, his dark eyes inquisitive. "Are you familiar with the basic difference between organic and rune-based magic?"

I pull a metal stool up to the tall granite table where he's standing. "Not really, sir."

He nods, unsurprised. "In short, organic magic is the power that comes from inside a witch, allowing her to control elements directly. For example, summoning witch fire, or brewing up a storm, all tap into organic power. Because organic magic reflects your internal state, it is highly volatile and requires a great deal of personal control and discipline to be used safely. The physical regimen of the school is here for a reason, Samantha. And though I understand athleticism is not entirely your forte—"

I clear my throat. "Not my forte" is a generous way of putting it.

"Nonetheless," Victor continues, "controlling your body helps you control your magic. Control that you, my dear, utterly lack."

"Not much for false praise, are you, sir?" I mutter.

"Flattery never fully goes out of style, my dear, but you do seem to like a direct approach. Now, as I was saying, you are not ready to touch organic magic yet. However, rune-based magic is much more controlled. It's about one single spell at a time. I have one I would like you to practice."

Reaching inside his coat, Victor pulls out a sheet of paper

that looks to have been cut with a razor from an old volume, the paper smelling of dust and age.

"This is a closing rune," Victor explains. "If drawn correctly on a locking mechanism, it engages the lock. Once you conquer a simple locking mechanism, we will move on to a more complex one."

With those instructions and an admonition to practice here each evening before we meet again next week, Victor leaves me, the instructions, and a box of locks in the lab. My curiosity as to why I might need a whole box disappears when, two hours into nothing happening, the first of my locks simply freezes in place as if the metal melted.

"Weren't you supposed be working at Dusk tonight?" Mika asks me when I return to the room close to midnight. She's buried deep in her laptop, those huge old-man glasses perched on the tip of her nose. I'm honestly impressed that she remembers what day it is, much less my schedule.

"I don't think I'm Cassis's favorite person right now." My chest tightens as I remember Victor's goons destroying Cassis's piano, the innocent baby grand cracking into pieces before our eyes. I don't know whether vampires can cry, but I swear I saw Cassis's eyes glisten. To make matters worse, I've just willingly spent an evening with the very male who destroyed it. A new wave of guilt races through me, tightening my stomach into knots —until Reese's words whisper through my mind. *It's not your fault.*

It's not my fault. Someday, I'll get up the nerve to go see how Cassis is doing, but until then, I have a big fat new fish to fry.

I plop onto my bed, fatigue weighing down my body. I consider telling Mika what I was doing, but find myself not wanting to talk about it, a warm, comforting gauze drifting over my mind as I fall asleep.

~

THE FOLLOWING DAY, I return from lunch to discover my room filled with boxes. Big ones, little ones, irregularly shaped ones —all piled up high enough that I can't see Mika at all, and only know she's there because I can hear her typing.

"Who vomited cardboard all over the place?" Digging my way to my desk, I'm grateful to discover that, despite their size, the parcels are light.

"From someone who wants you back at work." Mika calls, an annoying smile in her voice. "There's a note on the top box on the left."

"You read my mail?" I ask, finally able to see her.

She blinks and looks up from her screen, lowering her massive headphones. "It wasn't password protected. That's practically an invitation."

"It's on paper." I wave the envelope in proof.

"Well, that isn't my fault now, is it?"

Rolling my eyes, I read the note inside.

I expect you back at work today. Cut wages for missing yesterday. PS. Wear something nice.

Cassis. Apparently, I'm not as persona non grata as I thought. "What's inside the boxes?" I ask Mika.

"Why would I open your boxes?" Mika sounds indignant. "That's like burglary."

"Burglary is when you actually take shit. You have the weirdest moral code in the known universe." Grabbing a pair of scissors, I start by opening the first neat brown cube and pull out a small black silk...thong. The next box holds a tiny white bandage crop top. A fuck-me set of high heels. Skintight leather pants. Even a plaid skirt that looks like my uniform except with a flirty flair that turns it more toward naughty-schoolgirls porno.

Mika's eyes brighten. "So, which one are you going to wear?"

"None." I close the boxes back up, wondering how I'm going to get them back to Cassis. I can't go back to Dusk, no matter how much I want to. Not after what happened. Cassis might forgive me, but I'm still working on forgiving myself.

"You missed one," Mika says, tossing the last box toward me, this one much smaller than the others.

I consider just putting it atop the rest without opening it, but I'm not that virtuous. I can at least enjoy looking at the pretty things, even if I'm not going to keep them.

Opening the parcel, I discover this one holds not scant clothing, but the latest-model iPhone, a rakish picture of Cassis already set as the lock screen background. The message icon blinks with enough insistence to set off an epileptic seizure—definitely not the thing's default setting.

I click it.

Just in case you were thinking of quitting before your debt is paid, I'm picking you up. -C.

"Fuck me," I mutter.

"Not tonight, luv," a self-assured voice informs me from the door. "Though I do approve of where your mind is going."

16

Sam

*M*ika blushes and presses herself deeper into her computer screen as Cassis saunters inside our room and looks about with a small frown marring his perfect features. He wears a simple white shirt open to his sternum and sleeves rolled up to reveal corded forearms, fitted blue dress pants, and his dark hair slicked back from his forehead in a rakish old-Hollywood style that makes him look unbearably handsome. "I was rather hoping to see these decorating your body by now." He thoughtfully holds up a silk bralette. "But dress as you choose. So long as you get yourself into the car."

"Cassis." All the air in my lungs seems to somehow disappear. If I got hurt the way he did, would I be walking into my room right now? Courting more problems? Yet here he is, all broad shoulders and mischief and fierce rebellion. "You can't possibly want me at Dusk after——"

"If you think one pompous Godfather-wannabe arse is

going to bully me into getting rid of my worst bartender, you are sorely mistaken."

"You think I'm your worst bartender?"

"Absolutely." Cassis waggles his brows. "But you should come prove me wrong."

I laugh in spite of myself.

Cassis reaches out toward me, the air suddenly thick. My body tingles, the anticipation of his fingers brushing my cheek sending waves of heat along my skin. It's fucking unfair how beautiful he is, how much my body longs for him.

I swallow.

He pulls his hand back and straightens his rolled-up sleeves, as if that were his intention all along—though the tension in his eyes says it wasn't. "I'll wait for you in the car." Cassis turns toward the door as abruptly as he came in, fluttering a hand back toward Mika. "Bring the tiny sidekick if you want. Just get there."

I sigh. For some crazy reason, he wants this. And I owe him. That's all there is to it.

Going back through the boxes, I pick out an outfit at random, ending up in surprisingly comfortable black leather skinnies that fit my curves perfectly (that part's not surprising, knowing Cassis), black stiletto booties, and a tight silvery-gray crop top. I pull my own leather jacket on last. If Cassis doesn't like it, he can bite me. The jacket and I have a history.

When I look in the mirror to brush on some mascara and pearlescent highlighter from the Sephora box and put on giant silver hoops from the Tiffany's box—which I'd bet my ass are actually platinum—Mika whistles behind me. "You look like Trinity from *The Matrix*."

I roll my eyes.

Five minutes later, Mika and I are at the drive-up

roundabout in front of the Academy, staring at Cassis's gleaming red Lamborghini.

The vamp watches me as we walk toward him, his dark eyes trained on my body with so much force, I nearly trip.

He opens the back door for Mika, then turns to me, boxing me in against the car for a moment. His rich male musk drifts into my lungs on the evening breeze. With one last lingering look up my body, from my legs to the sliver of skin at my stomach to my eyes, he says, "Divine."

Then he opens the door for me and walks around the car, leaving me a hot, trembling mess.

"I thought you drove a Corvette," I say, settling against the leather seat, trying to keep the sudden breathiness from my voice.

"I run on many cylinders." Pressing the gas, Cassis turns out onto the main road, checking the rearview mirror. Thick walls of pines flash by on either side. "Did your shadow bring a laptop to my bar? I don't know whether to be horrified or insulted."

"Just be happy she isn't asking to set up a server in one of the booths."

"Actually, I was going to see if—" Mika starts.

"No," Cassis and I both say at the same time.

Once we get to Dusk, which is alive with its usual evening merriment, classic big band jazz pumping from the speakers, Mika settles into a corner to people-watch—or vamp-watch—while I head toward the bar—and stop. There, on the raised stage where Louise, Cassis's old baby grand once stood, is a brand-shining-new instrument. A gleaming black Steinway grand, even larger and more overpowering than the last.

A corner of Cassis's mouth rises proudly. "What do you think, luv? She doesn't have quite the same personality as Louise, but we're getting to know each other."

"She is beautiful, Cassis," I say, running my fingers over the smooth surface. And I mean it. However the vamp got a new piano onto the island so quickly, he did not skimp on quality. "Did you name her too?"

The vamp's eyes drop to half-mast. "I have."

I wait.

Nothing.

Fair enough. Cassis doesn't owe me anything. It's me who owes him—starting with an apology and a promise.

Squaring my shoulders, I turn toward him and grip his dark brown eyes with my own. "Listen. I...I want you to know that what happened last weekend with Victor, it won't happen again. I'm learning vampire etiquette now, and I can muddle my way through the basics easily enough. This is a vamp club, and you know, when in Rome. Anyway. I just wanted you to know."

Instead of easing, Cassis's normally mischievous eyes flash with anger before he hides it just as quickly. "Whose little idea was it to teach you vamp etiquette?" he asks quietly. "And exactly how did they go about it?"

"Mine." Walking up beside me, Reese crosses his large arms over his chest, his lips pressed together as he studies Cassis. I'm shocked to see him in something other than fatigues or exercise clothes—a black suit that hugs his tall body perfectly, his dark hair tidied back into a low knot. His blue eyes gleam with warning out of his sculpted face, making my throat dry. "And I went about it exactly the way you might imagine."

Heat fills me as Reese's commanding voice brings back all too many memories. Very vivid memories. Making things a thousand times worse, I see Cassis's nostrils flare delicately as his gaze cuts to me.

Fucking vampires with their fucking sense of smell.

Collecting what remains of my dignity, I raise my chin, turn on my heels, and march myself behind the bar to take orders.

Over the next two hours, Dusk hits its stride. My hands fly over the backlit liquor shelves to fill orders as the thong-clad vamp dancers mount their pedestals and gyrate to the music, every movement preternaturally graceful. The large screens all over the bar magnify each dancer's best moves, adding splashes of color to the image. Everyone is up dancing or drinking or both. Even Reese is nursing a whiskey that Cassis put in front of him. Everyone, that is, except for Mika, who huddles happily in her dark booth with her laptop for company, sipping a huge Diet Coke through a straw.

Then comes the moment of the night that anyone who is a regular at Dusk knows to wait for, as Cassis adjusts his cuff links and sits down at the piano. I put down the bottle I'm holding, a little rush of anticipation tickling my neck as the vampire's long pale fingers stroke the keys lovingly and Eddy Arnold's *Anytime You Are Feeling Lonely* echoes through the room.

I close my eyes for a moment, letting the music roll over me, my feet carrying me closer to the piano. No one is going to be ordering anything now anyway. Not while Cassis is playing.

Anytime you're feelin' lonely, the music sings, each note begging for vocals to join in.

Something cool and metal brushes against my hand, and I open my eyes to see someone thrusting a microphone into my hand, Cassis's deep chocolate eyes on mine.

My heart stops, then starts again at a gallop, adrenaline spilling into my blood. Sing. Cassis wants me to sing in front of everyone. And I suddenly can't remember how to open my mouth. The music races toward the start of the lyrics, and I know that in one more heartbeat, I'll miss my chance.

My gaze darts around the room, taking in the many, many

eyes all on me, the spotlight that someone adjusted to bathe me and Cassis.

A few feet away, Reese crosses his arms. When our eyes meet, he shakes his head. *Don't do it,* he mouths. *Do NOT bring more attention to yourself.*

My fingers fiddle with the mic.

No! Reese mouths again, somehow making the silent command boom inside me.

And that's all it fucking takes for me to find my spine. Drawing a deep breath just in time, I dive into the opening notes, the microphone carrying my clear soprano voice throughout Dusk. Glasses freeze in midair, mouths falling slightly open. I ignore them, letting my vocal cords warm to a gift I haven't given them in too long. At the piano, Cassis gives me an approving grin, playing more softly to accommodate my voice.

Anytime you're feelin' lonely
Anytime you're feelin' blue
The music pumps through my veins in sweeping beats.
Anytime you feel downhearted
I sing openly, barely avoiding a stumble as a low voice suddenly joins in. A rich, perfectly trained voice that makes every hair on my body stand on end. Reese—*Reese*—steps up beside me with a microphone in hand. Our gazes meet, his ice and my fire clashing into steam. He's trying to take some of the attention off me, but fuck it, with his voice, it's pot meet kettle.

Cassis, not one to waste an opportunity, improvises a mischievous little interlude as Reese and I both bring the mics up together.

That will prove your love for me is true
We sing, each voice opening as if in battle. The irony of the song's lyrics is not lost on me as the vamp and I face each

other, the microphones surrogate weapons of will. My heart keeps time as everything but the song and music and Reese blur to irrelevance around me. At my side, my free hand squeezes into a fist, my body flowing all my strength to my lungs. My voice. My sound.

Endorphins spill into my blood until I'm drunk on them. I only realize that the song's final notes have sounded when the room falls into silence. The music's lingering notes hang in the air, the whole of Dusk seeming to hold still as my chest heaves, my eyes locked on Reese's, on his stunned face.

The vamp's grip is tight around the microphone, his broad chest expanding with slow, rare breaths. My heart pounds so fiercely against my ribs that, given vampiric hearing, I am certain the whole of Dusk hears its instant *lub-dub, lub-dub, lub-dub.*

Clapping starts slowly somewhere in the back, more and more hands coming together to fill the tense silence.

Reese's microphone lowers, and he takes a step toward me, his tangy ocean-breeze scent filling my lungs.

My body responds without checking in with my mind. I can't think. Not drunk as I am on the music and feeling, on the applause. On Reese's scent. I swallow, the rest of the world disappearing except for the lines of Reese's strong face, his rebellious dark hair framing an angular jaw, his blue eyes more open and vulnerable than I've ever seen them.

Reese reaches out toward me, his fingers cool as they brush a stray bit of red hair behind my ear.

Distantly, I notice the club filling with sound again, the beat of dance music, shouts, and laughter. The spotlight turns off. But I'm still caught here in the shadows with Reese.

My breath stalls, the male's snowflake-light touch waking every nerve in my body. Despite all the eyes lingering on us, I can't resist tracing Reese's long lashes with my gaze, the scar at the corner of his mouth that betrays the violence I know filled his life.

With his same gentleness, I run my thumb over the tightness along his forehead.

Reese stills, his hand grabbing my wrist. The front of his trousers is bulging so hard that he must be in pain, pressed against the zipper like that. "You are a soul-shattering soprano."

"Thank you." I bite my lip, my thighs slick with arousal, which the sudden flare in Reese's nostrils says he smells perfectly well.

"Hades take me," Reese mutters under his breath and, gripping the back of my head, seals his mouth over mine.

I gasp, my lips opening to welcome him inside, but the vamp is not looking for a welcome. He sweeps in with a powerful tongue that claims my mouth with each stoke, all hesitation gone like a snapped rubber band. Deeper. Darker. Hotter. Each demanding sweep through my mouth sending zings of sensation to my breasts and sex and toes, my body aching with need.

Unable to contain the energy Reese's kiss sends rocketing though me, I rake my nails over his steely biceps. A groan I feel more than hear vibrates from his chest. His hand tangles in my hair, the slight pain from his harsh grip somehow feeding my pulsing arousal. By the time his mouth releases me, I so weak-kneed that his hold is the only thing keeping me up.

Holy fucking fuck. All that. From a kiss.

Cassis, asshole that he is, starts playing again under the house music. This time, it's "God Save the Queen."

17

Sam

I kissed Reese. *I kissed Reese.* The memory hits me over and over the rest of the night, each time feeling like a new revelation. I kissed Reese. He kissed me. And then... I went back to the bar, and Reese went wherever he went. He didn't come over to say goodbye before leaving, only asked Mika to remind me that our 6:00 a.m. training the following day was still on.

"Well, did you want him to cancel it?" Mika asks reasonably as I groan and rub sleep out of my eyes the next morning, pulling on my training clothes with more force than necessary. I barely slept, the lingering phantom of Reese's lips arousing me all over again each time I closed my eyes. My friend frowns. "I thought Reese was still under Victor's directive to teach you vampiric etiquette, and it isn't the kind of thing you can learn in a night. Or a year. Trust me, I started when I was three, and I still bow wrong."

"He is. And no, I didn't want him to cancel. Fuck it. I don't know what I want. But it wasn't him kissing me and then hauling ass out of Dusk without saying goodbye." I snort, shaking my head at my own words. I sound like a naïve high schooler, confusing a kiss with a proposal. In fact, now that I think about it, Reese did the right thing.

It was late, and we were drunk on music. We had a moment. It was thong-drenchingly good. And then it was over. Just like the other hundreds of kisses I'm sure Reese has experienced over the centuries.

The kiss didn't change either of us. Nor does it change the fact that he's my superior and has ordered me to do something. Nor the fact that I don't like studying vampire etiquette at six o'clock on a Sunday morning. Hell, after what Sienna did to the vamp, I'm amazed Reese can still look at a witch, much less kiss one, even if it was only for the thrill of the moment.

Despite my rather convincing self pep talk, anxiety still prickles my body as I walk across the cool, misty green to the training room.

Reese isn't there yet, so I take a few swipes at the hanging punching bags, my gaze sliding along to the clock on the wall. 6:02 a.m. My stomach clenches. The male is two minutes late now. And Reese is never late. He's got that whole military "if you're not early, you're late" stick up his ass.

I kick the bag again, the minute arm sliding to 6:05, and wonder how long I should wait before acknowledging that the male has no intention of showing up. Probably because I was wrong—it's not that he thought last night was nothing, it's that he actively regrets it. Or he's simply decided that I'm not worth his time.

Which would not be an altogether bad thing.

I don't want to impose on Reese's time, and I sure as hell don't want him imposing on mine. In fact, the farther I can keep away from Reese and Ellis and any other male, the better off I'll be. Isn't that the most important lesson I taught Janie before leaving for Talonswood? Trust no one. Let yourself be dependent on no one. You are in charge of you. Always.

You'll need help navigating this world, Sam, Reese's voice warns me. I shudder. The male wants me to lower the high wall that I've built so carefully around myself for the past twenty years.

I shrug him away. *It won't be that easy, Reese.*

"The answer is still no, Jack." The door to the training room opens, and Reese strides in with a phone against his ear, my chest tightening despite myself. From the exasperated look on his face, he's been at this conversation for some time. "I'm dead, remember? Lose this phone number for a few more years. I have an important meeting. Goodbye." Clicking the phone off, Reese stuffs it into the side pocket of a gym bag he carries. "My apologies, Samantha. I had—doesn't matter. Take off your shoes. We won't be working on vampiric etiquette today." His voice is as cool and collected as always.

Right. Good. We aren't talking about anything. It must have been two other people who sang a duet and made out last night.

I pull off my sneakers at the edge of the mat. Reese toes his off across from me. He's wearing slim black joggers today and a sleeveless shirt, putting the tribal tattoos running up his arm on full display. Along with his large muscular arms, so sculpted, they are fit for anatomy study.

"What are we working on?" I ask.

Reese locks the training room door. "On how to get away from an attacker. I believe Ellis started you on this, so we'll pick up from whatever you remember."

I blink as I try to recalibrate my priorities. "Is there someone coming after me?"

"I imagine the thought has crossed the mind of at least half the vamps who were at Dusk yesterday. We *are* predators. And you..." Reese straightens, his hard body moving with predatory slowness, each muscle a leashed cord of violence. "You are too damn tempting."

"Was that...a compliment?"

"No. It's reality, Samantha. You are beautiful, and you are a witch. A volatile combination that, as Quinn and Bernadette have proven, drives otherwise sane people to do things that they should not."

"Would we call Quinn sane?"

"Focus," Reese snaps. "You're an exotic curiosity. It's time you learned to defend yourself like one."

Heat races through me, and not the good kind. The number of things wrong with what Reese just said... "I'm an exotic curiosity that corrupts nice little vamps like Quinn into doing misdeeds." I yank off my socks, flinging them to the corner of the mat. "Well, good to fucking know. Let me apologize for corrupting *you* yesterday, Lieutenant. Apparently, that lust spell I've been brewing finally worked."

"Samantha—" Reese cuts himself off with a sigh. He rubs his eyes wearily with one large hand, but by the time it lowers, something has hardened inside him, his sapphire gaze cooling to ice. "First. Do not speak lightly of your magic again, and do not dare jest about using it on me." He draws a breath. "Second—yes. Yes, you are an exotic curiosity." The words carry a finality to them, the vamp doubling down on his insulting idiocy. "Yes, you are bloody tempting. And yes, you are the sole member of a species that many of the vamps remember less than fondly. So you might as well stop whining and start training, because you're in a dangerous place whether you think it's fair or not. Victor and his tricks are only the beginning. Many are going to come after him, wanting things from you, expecting things from you, and you are going to have to learn to keep a cool head."

Wait, now I'm *whining?* My hand curls into a fist, my knuckles itching oh so hard to sink into Reese's jaw. The male of last night seems dizzyingly far away, I almost think I must have imagined him.

His gaze flickers to my clenched fist. "Go ahead and try it." The sneer on his face seeps into his voice. "See how that ends for you."

I snort and loosen my fingers, the rage flowing through my blood flashing from hot to cold. "You aren't worth hitting, vamp."

He shrugs a powerful shoulder, my words rolling right off him like the insignificant mortal blip that I am.

"We'll start with basic grip escapes." Reese's fingers wrap around my wrist, that zing of electricity shooting through me at the touch. Plainly, my body never got the Reese-is-an-asshole message. He tightens his grip, my wrist small in his callused hold. "Work against the thumb. Start."

Fine.

Jaw set indifferently, I practice the motion, twisting my forearm from Reese's harsh hold. It's fucking demoralizing since I know I'm not *actually* escaping anything—Reese is simply releasing me when he's decided the effort is good enough. Except there are no effort trophies in the real world. Ellis and Quinn have already shown me what immortals can do, and I know that no matter how good I get at escaping holds or kicking in just the right way, I could never overpower an immortal.

Magic, however… That's the equalizer. I hold on to that thought as a bruise spreads across my forearm, my skin red and sore from escaping Reese's hold over and over. I worked on the closing rune Victor gave me all day yesterday, alone in the chem lab while every other cadet was out enjoying their liberty, and can seal a simple lock closed one out of three times now. Small step, but a start. There are more rune spells than that. And one day—one day, I won't be relying on an asshole to decide the moment my wrist should be released.

Reese's foot sweeps my ankle, and I fall hard onto the mat, the room blinking around me.

"Pay attention, witch," he barks. "Because I can keep tossing you down on your head all morning."

Heat pulses through me. "You can keep tossing me on my head as long as your vampiric strength lets you," I snap, hopping back to my feet and extending my arm again. It might be futile, but like hell am I giving Reese the satisfaction of seeing me cower. My chest heaves, anger and fatigue melding together. "If you actually wanted to help me defend myself, you'd help me flex my magic, not my bicep."

"You can't control yourself, and you want to control *magic*?" Reese snaps right back at me, his nostrils flaring, his usually pale face taking on color. "Did you lose your mind? We don't hand soldiers nuclear weapons and say, here, see if this works better for you than a handgun—no need to fucking aim. You think you're any different?"

"You clearly think you are." I step into Reese's space and shove him as hard as I can. The male doesn't move an inch, which only infuriates me further. Especially since angry Reese is sexy as hell, his angular jaw clenched, his already chiseled muscles all tense and quivering with power. I raise my chin. "You use your vampiric strength all the time and then have the gall to stand there saying I shouldn't be doing the same. Because God forbid we stand on the same footing."

The growl escaping Reese's chest tells me how far I've gone, but I'm just reckless enough to keep going. "You know what you've been teaching me?" I snarl into his face. "How to bend a knee and gratefully accept whatever scraps you wish to offer."

18

Sam

"Scraps?" Reese's voice rises, filling the gymnasium, his broad shoulders spreading. Taking up space and air in a way that makes my sex clench alongside my fists. The vamp takes a step forward, looming over me, one unruly black lock slipping over his forehead. "If that's what you think I've been teaching, you weren't paying attention."

I shove him away, and this time, he condescends to back up a step, his blue eyes flashing fire.

"What do you imagine you're going to do, witch?" Reese demands, his wide chest all but begging to be shoved again.

I'm already in motion when I realize the asshole set me up, grabbing my wrists as I come forward and using my momentum to spin me around. The next moment, he slams my chest into the nearby wall. The scent of cool vinyl fills my nose, mixing with Reese's minty ocean tang.

Anger courses through me as the vampire's presence surrounds me completely—and my own unwanted arousal.

There's something about him pressing me against the wall, his chest heaving, his control strained to breaking, that makes me wet as hell. "I imagine you're a prick," I yell, though with my face squished against the padded wall, it comes out garbled. "A prick who can't decide what he wants."

"Says the fountain of wisdom who's been alive for how long?" Reese growls into my ear. "Has it occurred to you for one damn moment that maybe you don't have the whole world figured out? That maybe you should shut up for a bloody second and learn?"

I yank against his unforgiving hold. There's no give. Not with how he's pinned my arm behind me, making any motion painful, his powerful control sending white-hot streaks of need down my spine. I want him. Correction, my body wants him. Fortunately, I'm not going to let my body do the thinking. "Learn that you are stronger than me? I think you've made that plain enough."

Reese twists me around to face him, now pinning my biceps to the padded wall. "You have no idea of your own power," he says, filling up every bit of air in the world. "But you are too *you*, and blind and naïve to know the responsibility that—"

"Go to hell, Reese." I aim my knee right into the large bulge pulsing in the front of his training pants. Given the size of the target, I fully expect not just to hit it, but to make the shot count.

Reese twists with vampiric grace, taking my shot on his thigh. "Been there, doing that." His mouth is so close to my face that the words tickle my skin. Pressing me harder into the wall, he kicks my ankles apart, taking my balance until it's only his grip that's holding me upright.

And fuck me if I don't like it.

I bare my teeth. "And apparently burned away half your soul in the fl—"

His mouth seals over mine, and I kiss him back hungrily, my head swimming. Somewhere deep in my chest, the buzz of magic awakens to Reese's presence, making every sensation a thousand times more potent, especially his dizzying taste.

I want to kill him. I want him inside me. I want this kiss to never end. I want it over. I can't think. I only want. Need.

My nails rake over the male's skin, leaving gashes in their tracks, and he growls against my lips.

His hand tangles in my hair, his mouth hard and punishing enough to leave my own bruised. I don't care. I have things I want to say to him too. And the gloves are coming off.

Reese pulls away as suddenly as he came to me. A scream catches in the back of my throat as he steps away and, in a lightning-fast blur, roundhouse-kicks the closest punching bag clear off its hook. Spinning back on me, the vampire grabs my hips and fucking lifts me into the air until our eyes are level. Until I see the blue flame and need roaring in his gaze.

"You have three heartbeats to get the hell out of here, witch," he says, the words straining to his throat. "Otherwise..." His gaze shoots to the punching bag, now lying on its side. The hoarseness of his voice, coupled with the hard bulge between his legs, leaves no doubt of his intention.

"I think I'm done taking orders from you." I wrap my arms around his neck and my legs around his waist, digging my heels into his hard backside so hard that he groans. It's my turn to take his mouth. No asking, no permission. My tongue strokes his, taking command.

And I'm airborne before I can draw my next breath, lungs emptying with a whoosh as I land stomach down on the overturned punching bag. I gasp like a fish, my head spinning with primal need.

Reese lands behind me, one powerful hand pressing down into my back. With a harsh shove, he rolls me forward over the bag until my ass is high in the air.

A ripping sound fills my ears as my training pants are shredded off me. Bare from the waist down, bent ass up over a punching bag. Pinned. The sudden vulnerability of the position has me rearing back, but Reese's steel hand holds me easily in place. The restraint only drives my arousal higher, making my breath come in sharp pants.

Moisture drips from my sex, slithering along my heated skin.

Reese rubs his hands along both my thighs, slathering them in my wetness as if it were fucking hand lotion.

My cheeks flame. "You're an asshole, Reese."

His hand lifts off my ass and comes down with a hard smack.

"Fuck!" I scream. Fire explodes across my right cheek.

He slaps the other side, but this time, I groan, the pain transforming into blinding pleasure. I arch my back and push back against him, begging for more.

I feel something hard press against my entrance. Hard and large and slippery wet. My hips rise to meet it.

With a growl, Reese pins me down and sheathes himself inside me in a single stroke that makes me scream.

The invasion is so complete, all I can do is gasp for breath.

With Reese inside me, I feel the tension in his body as he stills, letting my channel adjust to the great size of him. Except I don't want him to wait. Don't want to adjust. I want him to fucking take me already.

I open my mouth to curse him again, but Reese beats me to it, thrusting deep with a hard groan. Again. Again. He finds a punishing rhythm, pounding into me with precision too perfect to be human, every delicious stroke making my channel clench and pulse for more. I gasp for breath, wet slaps of his sac striking my skin echoing shamelessly through the training room.

I take every hard thrust, unable to move beneath Reese's shackling hold, unable to do anything but feel.

Sam

*H*eat fills my core and pools in my channel, the little spot Reese's cock hits with every thrust singing from need.

The canvas rubs my clit each time he pounds into me, making me moan unintelligibly and grind my hips harder against it. Driving me closer and closer to the edge, faster than I've ever gotten there before.

The sensations are overwhelming. The friction of the bag, the rasp of his cock against my soaking, sensitive flesh, his callused hands gripping my hips with bruising vampiric strength.

Just like he bruised my wrist in training.

I stop cold for a split second, disbelief ricocheting through me.

Reese. Reese is inside me.

The same cold-eyed vampire who pinned my chest to the mat, who stood over me a week ago and screamed into my ear until I collapsed sobbing into the sand. Who ordered me to obey him in the shower. Just thinking about that makes my blood simmer even hotter, a cry falling off my lips as my hips undulate faster along his rock-hard length.

Reese punishing me. Reese pinning me down against this bag with unyielding hands. My breath comes in short, sharp gasps as the edge grows dizzily closer.

What's wrong with me? Am I fucked up to be so turned on by this? Last week, I barely knew this male and…and now I can't imagine him ever pulling out of me. The edge grows further away, my mind spinning with doubt.

"Stop thinking," Reese growls into my ear, halting my runaway mind in its tracks.

Before I can say anything, he pins me down harder. This time, his hand in the small of my back is so heavy that my hips have no room to move at all. Not even to undulate to the rhythm of his hard thrusts.

I struggle against the pressure—and feel a tiny, needle-sharp point brush my neck. I freeze, blood whooshing in my ears.

I hold still, afraid if I move, he'll stop. The pressure increases, making me mewl with want. I *want* him to bite me. I want him to take what he wants. I moan into the mat. Reese inhales sharply, then pulls away, seeming to collect himself.

Fuck me. This is so, so wrong.

"Wrong?" he echoes, and I realize that I spoke my thoughts aloud. A moment later, he slides out of me, and I whimper at the loss of him.

His palm comes down hard on my ass, turning the whimper into a yelp.

Shit. Oh, shit that hurt.

"I said, stop thinking," his voice rasps behind me. I gasp, inhaling the vinyl scent of the blue mat, my fingers raking along it. Reese lands a second slap, the sting focusing my mind on my burning ass.

Even as I clench in anticipation of what's to come, I welcome the fiery heat, the way it vibrates straight to my clit. Moisture slithers from my sex, slicking my skin and the punching bag I'm helplessly bent over.

When the next one lands, I scream with the impact, one breath away from the edge.

Reese yanks my hips up and flips me over so my back is flat on the mat, my half-naked body splayed out before him. He towers over me, more breathtaking than he's ever been, pale face sculpted with focus, blue eyes piercing mine.

The mountains of his shoulders and pecs ripple with tiny muscles as he braces his elbows on either side of me, surrounding me with his scent, his strength. Without warning, he shifts his hips to thrust deep into my channel. When I gasp, he takes my mouth, plundering it as he pounds into me, driving us up the vinyl mat, driving my need up, up, up. I scream against his lips and wrap my legs around him, using the leverage to slam my hips against his so the slaps echo off the gymnasium walls.

His mouth shifts, brushes the side of my neck, his cool breath waking my skin. Then I hear his fangs unsheathe, feel those sharp points again, trailing across my skin until goose bumps light up every inch of my body. I whimper, wanting more. More pressure.

"Samantha," he whispers, and his fangs just break my skin.

I scream, the wave of orgasm starting at my sex and shooting uncontrollably through my body. My muscles clench around Reese, my toes curling beneath the wave of pleasure so intense, it almost hurts, my channel spasming around his hard, pulsating cock. Again. Again. The aftershocks continue raking through me even as I gasp limply for breath, as Reese groans and his own release spills inside me.

After a long, gasping moment, he pulls out of me with a gentleness that is utterly unlike what we were just doing. Helping me up, he settles me with my back propped up against the punching bag and crouches before me, his brilliant blue eyes studying me intently. Damp dark hair frames his unfairly beautiful face, a thin sheen of sweat glistening on his forehead. Reaching out, he runs a thumb along my cheekbone.

"How are you doing, Samantha?" Reese's voice is a low rumbling caress that echoes through me.

"Reese—" I start to say and stop, not knowing what to say. That was... That was mind-blowing. Hot. So much so that... that I can't stop trembling even now from the storm of sensations raking through me. I shift, wincing as my sore ass presses into the floor.

Sore because Reese... Heat fills my cheeks.

The male smirks.

Fuck it. He knows exactly what I'm remembering. I shut my mouth without saying anything. Shut my eyes too, my heart picking up speed. The past half hour was incredible. The height of pleasure. Of intensity. And yet the things I let Reese do to me—the things I enjoyed him doing to me— they're not who I am. Certainly, they're not compatible with who I want to be.

The warm glow that has been tingling though my body plunges to ice, shame shoving every ounce of contentment from me. I let a man hold me down. Restrain me. Make me take him as he wanted. Reese ordered me around. He... spanked me. Hard.

What kind of person likes that? Loves it. What's fucking wrong with me that even the memory of his iron hold makes my head swim with arousal.

"I need to go," I whisper.

A flicker of pain crosses Reese's face, vulnerability flashing in his eyes before he buries it beneath that mask. "What's wrong, Samantha? Something changed. Talk to me."

Yes, no shit something changed. I came to my senses and found them not one bit happy with me. I push myself up, ignoring the hand Reese offers. Lifting a hand that suddenly feels heavy as lead, I brush the small spot on my neck where Reese just punctured my skin. A tiny smear of blood comes away on my finger. Yeah, to top off everything else, I not only let a vampire bite me, but found it hot instead of terrifying.

Reese watches me look at the blood, standing silently as he scans my face, trying to read what I'm thinking. "I didn't drink your blood, Sam. I would never do that without your permission."

My pants are a torn black mess in a corner of the mat. I pick them up and walk unsteadily over to my bag, pulling out the spare uniform skirt that I always keep in there.

It takes me three tries just to get my first leg into the skirt, Reese's hand twitching toward my elbow before I glare at him. The whole room seems cold now. Strange.

Reese brushes his hands over his face. "Talk to me, Samantha." The request turns to command, his British accent growing clipped. "Did I misread your body? Did you not enjoy what we did?" He holds very, very still, waiting for my reply.

"I enjoyed it fine." *That's the problem.* I turn my back to him to change my racerback tank for the uniform blouse from my bag. "I'm on birth control, in case you were worried," I say over my shoulder, my words dull.

"I know. I have your medical file."

Yeah. Of course he knew that. Reese knows everything about my own body better than I know it myself. "May I be dismissed, sir?" I ask without turning around.

Reese steps in front of me, cutting off my route. "You can tell me what the bloody hell just happened." His blue eyes flash at me, his hands opening and closing at his sides. "One moment you are wet and—"

"Stop!" Blood rushes to my cheeks. "I know exactly—" I cut off with an angry snap. I know well enough what I did without Reese spelling out my shortcomings for me again. Or maybe the vamp doesn't consider them shortcomings. Maybe in his world, that is how women are supposed to act. Submissive and happy about it. "I don't want to talk. I want to leave. May I do that, sir?"

"Sam—"

Grabbing my bag, I hurry out the door before waiting to hear the end of his sentence.

2 0

Reese

*R*eese tossed his phone onto Cassis's leather couch and stared at the glass of whiskey his brother—Cassis was his brother no matter what Reese had said to Victor —had placed before him. The liquid reflected the sparks of overhead light. Taking the glass, he downed the drink in a single shot.

"You are broody, even for you." Refilling Reese's glass, Cassis crossed his legs and leaned back in his chair. In black silk trousers and a French-cuff white shirt, the male looked positively polished—but Reese knew it was just another skin. Reese had been there in the centuries when Cassis's sword was the deadliest known, and the ones when Cassis had traded that sword for a scalpel and dove into medicine. And when Cassis walked away from that too. Dusk was the latest in the male's adventures. But Reese had to admit, when Cassis threw himself into something, he went all the way. And currently, Cassis had his sights set on him. "And if I'm going to be sharing my good whiskey," Cassis continued, taking a savoring sip of his own drink, "it seems only polite that you should share something in return."

Reese gave him a dark look.

"Do let me savor your pain, Reesand. I want all the gory details."

"I came here to get drunk, arsehole," Reese told him.

"Yes, about that." Cassis refilled Reese's glass, which was somehow empty again. "You are a vampire, I must remind you. The amount of alcohol it would take for you to get drunk…well… Let's just say you should settle in for a long night of effort before you can enjoy the effects of oblivion. On the bright side, it's wonderful for me from a business perspective."

Reese snorted. Cassis was not lacking for funds—none of them were. Hell, when you have investments with over six centuries of yield on them—especially when you make smart choices—well, there were advantages to immortality. None of which was currently of any help with the fact that he'd gotten ripped apart by a witch. Again.

"I took Samantha," Reese blurted.

"Took?" Cassis studied his whiskey. "Are we having trouble with words, or did the witch not participate in the decision?"

"Of course she participated," Reese was on his feet at once, the glass he'd been holding crushed to bits in his grip. The notion of forcing a female—any female—repulsed him. Samantha had wanted him. He had smelled her arousal as plainly as perfume. Hades take him, the way the witch's body had responded to him was enough to make him hard even now. The control it took to keep from ending things prematurely had strained Reese in a way he'd never felt before. Not even with… No. He wasn't going to think of his wife. Not now. Not when he could still feel the tightness of Sam's channel around his cock.

Bloody fucking hell. Reese walked to Cassis's window, looking out over the sparkling lights of downtown Talonswood.

He'd kept the memory of his wife alive for four hundred years precisely by avoiding entanglements like this one. The moment he'd given in to the temptation with Sam had felt like plunging off a cliff—terrifying, and probably just as deadly. This wasn't what he'd wanted. Just like their last lesson, when he hadn't meant to carry her broken body into his own shower and wash her clean. She did things to him. He walked in with one intention and walked out with his body and soul turned inside out.

The coupling had driven Reese insane. Made his head swim with want and need, and something more. Something even stronger than that.

When he had slid himself into Samantha, he'd felt a jolt of life energy shoot through him, taking away his rare breath. As if something long gone had returned for a spell, only to disappear again when Samantha turned her back on him. Reese still felt the reverberation of that blow.

"I let my cock get ahead of my common sense," he snapped at his brother. "Given that this is an everyday occurrence for you, I thought you'd understand."

"I take no one I care about to bed," Cassis replied.

Reese looked at Cassis for a long moment, then dropped himself back onto the couch. Yes. Yes, that was exactly the bloody problem. His body had roused to Samantha's since the moment he let her out of that damn limo in front of the Academy, the painful throbbing of his cock a regular companion anytime he looked at the girl too long. With the red streaks in her hair matching her fire-filled personality, those full breasts and full lips he couldn't help but imagine closing around his cock, Reese's anatomy hadn't stood a chance. But that was all it ever should have been. Anatomy. Physiology. Infuriating, but nothing more.

He should never have allowed himself to do anything as stupid as care.

Taking the witch to get his need for her out of his system would have been one thing. He knew he could ensure she enjoyed herself, and Hades take him, her body had responded to his like a tuned violin. Especially once he got that busy mind of hers to stop thinking so much. Fuck. Maybe that was where he'd gone wrong. He should never have allowed himself to savor Sam's plunge into discovering her pleasures, never tried to take her to the next level of trust and arousal. That type of thing created too much of a bond. Or the illusion of one.

Ironically, the joke was on him. Reese had poured too much of his soul into the whole thing, showed enough of himself to the witch to give her access to the part of him that could still be hurt. He hadn't meant to. But once he was inside her, it felt as though something inside him unlocked and wouldn't close again.

And when she'd turned her back on him at the end, all her body shouting her regret at having allowed him inside her, it had fucking hurt. Worse, the darkness that had settled around him when Samantha walked out of the training room was closing in more with every passing hour. Suffocating him.

"I think you are talking to the wrong creature," Cassis said, taking another sip of his whiskey. "Ellis appears to have lost whatever passes for his common sense after bedding Samantha as well. You two can get together and self-flagellate as a pair."

"The arsehole thinks you are connected to the witch as well, you know," Reese said. It was a jab, but he didn't care. Not with Cassis sitting there all smug and controlled as if he hadn't a care in the world. "You and me, and him and Asher. The whole horsemen foursome."

Cassis's face darkened, his eyes flashing. "No one made you stick your cock into a witch, brother." He finished his drink, setting the glass carefully back down on the table. "Not you, not Ellis. I think I'll make my own decisions as to what I do with that particular body part. Unlike you, I know when to let it do the thinking and when not to."

"You feel it, Cassis. The damn pull. That's why you have Samantha working at Dusk," said Reese.

Cassis shrugged one shoulder, his anger hidden as quickly as it had flashed.

Reese's gaze fell onto his phone, the screen flashing with yet another message from Jack. His hand went to the Delete button by habit, stopping a millimeter away just in time. His jaw tightened. Fuck it.

He got to his feet.

"Where do you think you're going?" Cassis asked. "You're still a good ways away from getting plastered, which I thought was the purpose of this little brooding session."

Reese grunted, his fingers busy asking Jack for coordinates. A moment later, the long lat coordinates lit up the screen, along with a *hope you still like sand*. Sand. Hmm. Sounded like the Middle East somewhere. Good enough. "Is your Cessna flight-ready?" he asked Cassis without looking up. "I need to borrow it."

21

Sam

*D*read follows me into the training room for the next scheduled training session with Reese. The conversations I've been practicing with myself all feel awkward no matter how many times I go over them in my head.

Except Reese is not there.

Asher is. With thick golden hair and tawny eyes, the male looks like he just stepped off the cover of *GQ*—except for the closed expression clamping down his features. His dislike of me is palpable enough to fill the room.

"Lieutenant Reesand has been called away," Asher informs me by way of greeting, his hard voice matching his face. "I've no one else I can spare for your individual instruction right now, so it will be put on hold."

His words hang in the air, laden with thick condemnation. As if Reese's sudden departure is my fault. I guess arithmetic is on Asher's side right now—I've gone through two instructors in as many months.

My stomach tightens, concern and relief washing through me at once. I was not in the least prepared to face Reese on the mats again. But apparently I'm just as unprepared for his absence. Studying Asher's face, I can't help wondering if he knows what Reese and I did the last time we were in this room. What would Asher think of me if he knew how much I enjoyed it? I study the male more closely, noting the crossed arms and tight jaw, and realize that I really don't want to know what he's thinking right now.

"With midterm exams starting next week, I expect you will have plenty of demands on your time," Asher says, turning on his heel and heading out the door.

"Wait! Where did he go?"

Asher pauses but doesn't turn. "That is his business."

"When will he be back?" I ask. "I mean, *will* he be back, sir?"

Asher walks out without answering.

WITHIN THE NEXT TWO DAYS, the reality of the coming midterms hits Talonswood Academy like a snowstorm. A certain quiet settles over the students, with books opened at mealtimes and conversations turning toward details of the fae-vampire wars and mathematical theorems. Blissfully, all this focus means that Christian, Wayne, and their cronies are finally too distracted to torture me.

I'm fine with Reese being gone. I'm happy he left before I had to face him again. Because whoever I was in that training room, I can't afford to be. I'm...I'm back to how things were when Victor had just taken over the place, before Reese and I had even exchanged words, much less bodily fluids.

That is to say, sleepless, on edge, and enjoying a front-row seat to whatever nightmares my mind comes up with each night. I've started waking up each morning with a small, nagging headache—lack of sleep will do that—but can usually suppress it with an ibuprofen or two.

"The vamps have an unfair advantage." Wayne is busy holding court with a group of the stronger demifae in the middle of the green. In their crisp white and blue uniforms under a clear blue sky, fall leaves skipping around them, they look like a poster for an American Ivy League college. I speed up as I pass them on my way to the chem lab—walking with a purpose creates the illusion that someone is waiting for you. That someone will come asking questions if you don't show up on time. Wayne growls, a deep, predatory sound that makes my skin crawl. "They need less sleep. Have more time to prep."

"True, but they have further to go," I mutter to myself. "Some need to learn to read first."

"What was that, Samantha?" Victor's cool voice makes me jerk to a stop, cursing myself for letting down my guard. A demi's hearing is better than a human's, but a full vamp's ears are downright dangerous. I should have seen him crossing the green toward me, two of his hulking vamp bodyguards trailing an almost-subtle distance behind him.

"Count Victor." I drop my eyes politely, my throat tightening for a moment at the fact that Reese, who taught me the difference between empty manners and true submission, has been gone for a week. "Good evening, sir."

Victor makes a noncommittal sound that I take to mean I'm allowed to raise my eyes. Around us, the green is quickly shifting into motion, cadets starting to notice Victor and immediately breaking up their clusters, looking as busy and studious as possible. Wayne and his group throw me dark glares, as if I'm somehow at fault for dispersing their gathering.

"I came to inquire about your progress with the closing spell I gave you. Have you found your way into practicing it?"

I give Victor an account of my progress, that I've been able to close some of the simpler locks without melting them about one out of four times. Nothing spectacular, but it feels shamefully good to have someone to talk about my magic with, even if that someone is Victor. When I ask about expanding my practice to include opening the locks back up, however, the count shakes his head emphatically.

"One step at a time, young witch," he says. "Closing and opening may sound like they are two sides of the same coin, but I assure you that one is infinitely more volatile and dangerous than the other. It's like the difference between a spoon and a knife, to use a human analogy." Victor checks his watch—a gold Cartier that had to have set him back at least twenty grand, I notice distantly. "Continue the assignments I give you and inform me when you are ready for me to review the progress in person."

Victor waves his long fingers, dismissing both the subject and further inquiries with brutal efficiency. "As it happens, I had a second reason for seeking you out. I will be leading a select group of first years on a tour of some of Talonswood's notable sites, including the famous gateway to Talon. You are welcome to join, if you would find that a convenient way to spend a few hours of liberty."

22

Sam

*I*t's tiki night at Dusk, which means the dancers are wearing flower garlands and bikinis instead of diamonds and thongs, and the bar is decorated with carvings of wooden statues. Not to mention that I'm more naked than usual—Cassis's request for the occasion—in cheeky shorts and a hot-pink strapless corset that makes my breasts spill over the top like a Victorian romance heroine. Huge pineapple earrings weigh down my earlobes, encrusted with what I'm pretty sure are genuine yellow diamonds and emeralds.

By the time weekend liberty rolled around yesterday, my small headache each morning had turned into a mild fever and a nagging migraine, both of which I managed to drown out with ibuprofen before my shift tonight. For all the ways Newark's foster system fucked up my life, it also put my immune system through boot camp. I don't remember the last time I had so much as a cold, much less the flu, so to get sick at Talonswood Reform is adding insult to injury.

"Are you sniffing me?" I look behind me to find Cassis's nostril flaring delicately over my shoulder as I practice mixing Dusk's new take on a Bloody Mary which one of the other bartenders warned me was getting popular. Unlike its namesake, this one involves actual blood. O negative. From a silver decanter. It's a precision kind of thing. I wave my hand at the vampire. "I'm warning you right now, if you're consider taking a sip from either the glass or me, I'll smack you."

"Promise?" Cassis purrs, making heat rush to my face.

Fuck.

"You shouldn't tease." Cassis straightens his cuff links, something flickering across his face before his voice drops. "And don't jest with vampires about taking sips of your blood, Samantha. You look good enough to eat—you don't need to remind them." The admonishment echoes back to the warning Cassis once gave me about the dangers of his kind. For all his cockiness, when the male gets serious, it's enough to send a shiver down my spine.

Suddenly, I want out. Out of Talonswood, out of this life. I want to go back to Newark and worry about corrupt cops and normal sleazy men. I had nothing there, but at least I knew who I was. Or thought I knew. Whatever. I want to be the old Samantha who never expected anyone to stay, who learned long ago never to get attached. But instead, I have only me. And a headache.

So I do what I always have—conjure a facade of confidence and hope that no one smells blood in the water.

"Here, peace offering." I add a final splash of O negative to my concoction and hold it out to Cassis. "Tell me what you think."

Cassis takes a sip and purses his lips. "I think it is an affront to O negative and Grey Goose both." Setting down the whiskey he's holding, he reaches over my shoulder and fills a fresh glass with cassis liquor—the drink he has designated as mine. Picking up both glasses, he gestures to one of the booths in the back of Dusk. "Stop torturing my clients and come entertain me instead."

"I'm working," I tell him. "And if you aren't going to drink this, I'll find a new victim."

"Last I checked, I was your boss," Cassis smiles at my glower. "Which means you are free to take my suggestion of a break as an order."

Following Cassis, I slip into the booth on the other side of him and take a sip of the sweet liquor before glaring. There are already too many thoughts brewing in my head without Cassis messing with me. At least he isn't playing the piano—we both know his music would mesmerize me the way his compulsion cannot. Interesting how neither Reese's nor Cassis's trick works on me. Interesting too that I can scratch Ellis with my nails where it usually takes a solid knife to slice into an immortal's skin.

The back of my head gives a twitch, the pressure behind my eyes building. I'm tired and I want to sleep. Well, not sleep, but rest. Rubbing my eyes, I give Cassis a weary sigh. "What do you want?"

"To know what happened with you and Reesand." Cassis relaxes back against the cushioned seat, his masculine scent of spice and sin filling the air between us. Instead of looking at me, his rich brown eyes study the swirls of whiskey in his glass, his mussed hair framing his face in a way that underscores every masculine angle. It's enough to make my sex clench—and I have no doubt the male knows it.

I brace my forearms on the table's edge and lean forward. "We fucked. He left."

No surprise touches his perfect features.

I take a sip of my drink. "Why exactly do you care?"

"That is actually a very good question," Cassis says thoughtfully. "And to be honest, I haven't the bloodiest idea."

The frank admission takes me aback for a moment. My gaze falls on my palm and the mark I have there. The same one that Sienna left on the horsemen. We're connected somehow, the males and I. But after what I felt with Reese, I don't think I like the connection. Not if it turns me into something I don't recognize.

"Reese and I had a spat about my using magic." Utter truth. The specific order of events leading to his departure is a whole other story—but if Cassis insists on talking to me today, then I'm steering. "Never mind that without it, everyone in the Academy is stronger than me. Even the fae who can't shift into full animal form can still toss me into a ditch without breaking a sweat."

"So you're interested in pursuing a mixed martial arts career?"

"What?"

"Or gang leader?" Cassis asks.

I rub my face, trying and failing to follow his train of thought. "Why would—"

"I have no notion as to why." Cassis takes a deep swig of his drink. "But plainly not being able to best demis in a fistfight has set a burr under your saddle, so I'm just going along with the premise."

I roll my eyes, shaking my head as I meet Cassis's gaze. "I don't want to get into a fight, but I sure as hell want to be able to get out of one without the help of the cavalry. And for that, I need magic. Which no one is willing to teach me except..." I hesitate, a voice urging me to keep my mouth shut.

"Yes?"

I shove the hesitation aside—and find that I finally can. The warm gauze doesn't drift over my mind, making me want to talk about anything else.

Suddenly, I remember something Reese said about vampire compulsion—that it fades with time and distance.

Goddammit. Of course the count compelled me not to talk about the magic—which only makes me more desperate to talk about it now.

"Victor gave me a rune to practice and the use of a lab to work in," I say, holding my breath as the dean's name hangs between us.

"Victor." Cassis's eyes narrow dangerously.

I swallow but raise my chin. Cassis has every right to despise me for crossing paths with the bastard, but of everyone I know, he is also the most likely to understand why I took the risk. "Victor," I confirm.

Thoughts too fast for me to read flash over the vamp's beautiful face, before it reclaims its signature nonchalance. "Continue."

Right. I release a breath I didn't realize I've been holding. "It isn't much as far as instruction goes, but it's more than I can get from anyone else. I'm not so stupid as to trust the count, but beggars can't be choosers either, and facts are facts: Asher threw out all the witch texts from the library, Ellis won't go near me, and Reese had a fit when I even brought up magic. So here we are."

"Bollocks." The vamp flicks an invisible bit of dust off his suit jacket. "Asher is a prick with a stick so far up his arse that it comes out his throat, but he certainly didn't order book genocide."

"I checked the library."

"The previous dean ordered Asher to get rid of the books, and like a good little soldier, he followed orders—but if I know the bastard, he probably found a way to get those texts to Talon instead of destroying them altogether. Mind you, there were no witches around at the time to make use of them."

I digest this piece of information for a second, but ultimately come to the same conclusion I started with. "Does it even matter why or how? Point being that Victor is the only one who has an instruction manual for my powers."

"Have you asked anyone else?" Cassis inquires. "Besides Reese."

"Someone like who?"

"Me, for starters." Cassis places his hands behind his head, a smug expression on his gorgeous face. "I've been known to acquire certain hard-to-find objects. For a price."

I laugh without humor. "I'm afraid the only thing I have to offer the devil is my soul, Cassis. And trust me, you don't want that."

Cassis's dark eyes suddenly shift with a smoothness that closes my throat. "Don't hurt Reesand," he says. It takes me a few heartbeats to figure out that he isn't joking. "When Sienna couldn't break him, she butchered his wife before his eyes. That did the trick. Reese has not let a female close to him since." Cassis leans forward, his dark eyes penetrating into me. "If all you'd done was *fuck*, Samantha, he wouldn't have left."

Cassis's words grip the air between us, my chest tightening further with each heartbeat. Unable to help myself, I trace the scar on my palm, which suddenly seems to tingle with responsibility. "I…" I don't know what to say to that. Fuck, I don't even know what to feel. "He isn't here," I say dumbly. "I don't even know whether he is coming back."

Cassis leans back lazily, releasing the tension as swiftly as it came. "Oh, he's coming back," he says, savoring a sip of whiskey before pulling a phone out of his pocket. Something that looks like a GPS tracking program flashes on screen for a moment. "The arse took my plane. And I always keep track of my things."

23

Sam

I'm shattering. Pain tears through my body, boiling my blood. Each breath is heavy, the herculean effort needed to move my limbs so not worth it. I—

"Sam!" Mika's voice splinters the darkness, and I sit up in my sweat-soaked bed to find my friend's pale face hovering over me. "You're burning up. I can feel it from across the room."

I rub my eyes, my forehead as hot as my headache. Lingering vestiges of a nightmare caress my subconscious and I shiver despite my temperature. "I forgot to take my meds last night," I say, feeling around for the bottle of water and extra-strength ibuprofen the infirmary dispensed for me. My shift at Dusk had ended at two in the morning, and I'd more or less collapsed into bed the moment I walked into the room.

Mika activates a chemical ice pack and lays it on the back of my neck. Outside, the sun is just creeping over the pines, nearly obscured by growing steel-bellied rain clouds. "I wish I had something positive to tell you, but they won't count the semester if you skip exams today, so..."

"I know." Checking the time, I decide I might as well get up for the day, and plod into a cool shower to help take the edge of the fever. To my surprise, the shower and ibuprofen actually work, and by ten in the morning, I feel only semi-zombielike as I join the herd of other first years filing into a large classroom, my skin warm and clammy, but manageable. Rain has just started pattering at the four tall windows, a perfect match to the general mood. The desks have been set up in well-spaced columns, SAT style, the whiteboard at the front of the room announcing that we're here for basic trig.

Just as the door to the exam room is about to close, Ellis walks inside and settles into the back row. He looks about how I feel, his pale blond hair pulled back in a lank bun, revealing a clammy face and deep shadows under his yellow eyes. Which must mean whatever is happening inside him is ten times worse. My stomach tightens, my hand longing to reach out to him even though I know the contact would be unwelcome. Not that I could even reach all the way to the back. Given that there's an empty seat right beside me, I can't help but think Ellis's choice is deliberate. Still, because I'm a stubborn idiot, I try to make eye contact with the male.

He takes out a knife and starts sharpening his number two pencil with it, the efficient *swish, swish, swish* of steel on wood silencing the already subdued room.

Hell, if trig fails him, Ellis will have a spear for small game.

The door opens, and Asher strides into the classroom together with one of the mathematics instructors to begin distributing the booklets. The commander is as put together as always, his golden hair and tawny eyes complementing tanned skin. Even when doing something as simple as handing out paper, he moves with a predator's grace, the muscles beneath his blue collared shirt shifting subtly. When he places my booklet down in front of me, his earthy sandalwood scent makes my lungs tingle.

Swallowing, I focus on my exam booklet. Light blue with a little sticker to declare it a virgin. Most schools have moved on to computer testing by now, but we're all sitting here with sharpened number two pencils and Scantron sheets, ready to fill in bubbles. Two rows in front of me, Mika is staring at her low-tech supplies with righteous indignation, but fortunately decides against voicing her thoughts aloud.

Asher delivers the basic warning about cheating with a quiet menace that puts the fear of hell into everyone in the room, starts the timer, and leaves. Thanking whatever deity that cares that I have one less distraction, I open my booklet and begin tormenting ratios.

And I don't look up again until there is a shuffle at the door, a new proctor walking in to patrol the rows.

Reese.

My heart stutters, the pencil lead breaking against my desk as I stare at his perfect, closed-off face. In place of his usual clothes, the vampire is wearing desert-colored military fatigues with rolled-up sleeves and a tan shirt underneath, all streaked with dirt and dried blood. Just like his tan combat boots. His unruly hair is pulled away from his face, the tattoos on his arm wrapping the biceps in barbed wire. Wherever the male was, he's only just come back. And he came here first.

I stare at him over the bent heads of all the students, my heart pounding against my ribs.

He scans, trains his blue eyes on me, and walks down the rows toward me, every step of that perfect powerful body as lithe as a panther. Confident and powerful and panty-soaking perfect. Just as he was that night when he played my body and made me scream with mind-numbing pleasure for all the wrong reasons. I can't look away, can't stop hearing Cassis's words either. There is nothing about Reese that looks remotely soft or vulnerable, not unless I look deep into those haunted blue eyes.

"Is there a problem, Devinee?" he asks as he stops beside my desk, his voice cool and measured.

Yes, of course there's a problem. "No," I say softly, unable to tear my gaze from his. "No, sir."

Reese nods curtly as if there was nothing strange in our exchange at all and continues patrolling the desks while I remain rooted to my seat and unable to think. So much for no distractions.

As I take the test, I notice distantly that the room is actually starting to feel chilly instead of muggy. When I put a hand to my forehead, it's dry and cool, no trace of a fever.

Unfortunately, feeling better does nothing for my trig skills. I'm filling in the "b" bubble on all the multiple-choice questions I didn't get to just as the math professor returns to announce the end of the exam and collect the booklets. Before I can hand in my work, Reese walks out the door without a backward glance.

The exam room empties quickly after that, the cadets eager to be free of the oppressive walls, but I stay in my seat, my mind firmly on Reese. On what Cassis said to me last night. One part of me is determined to hunt Reese down. Another part has no idea what I'd say if I found him. As my fingers drum the polished surface of the desk, a sickly cologne scent reaches my nose.

"Witch bitch." Christian's foot jets out from behind me, hooking the leg of my chair and yanking hard.

The chair sways, my nails scraping helplessly over the table as I fall backward, landing with a crash. A dull sort of echo reverberates through me, and, before I can scramble up, Christian's foot presses my wrist into the floor.

"You think you are so very special, don't you?" The demivamp's face is twisted with disgust. "Spreading your legs for the count, like the slu—"

Suddenly Christian is yanked off me by his shirt collar with a gargling shriek.

I hear a growl, a crack, and jump to my feet in time to see Ellis striding toward the door, Christian holding his bleeding mouth. Flipping Christian off, I hurry after the fae. For a guy who's just come to my rescue, he still seems strangely unwilling to meet my gaze, his long legs carrying him quickly down the corridor and into the men's room.

As if that's going to stop me.

I catch the still-swinging door and follow Ellis inside. The one other person already in there, a skinny brown-haired second year, stares at me wide-eyed, his cock hanging out of his pants.

"What—" the boy starts to say.

"Leave," Ellis and I tell him together before glowering at each other.

The boy quickly tucks himself back into his pants, half skipping to the exit.

"You too," Ellis tells me, towering over me as he holds open the door. "Now."

"No." I'm not backing away, not this time. Walking calmly toward the marble countertop, I pull myself up to sit on it. "You look like shit, by the way. Or like you've become a vamp."

"What do you want?" Ellis asks. Despite his powerful frame, he looks pale, a thin sheen of sweat glistening at his temples.

"To apologize." I long to touch him. To help him. Fuck,

I'd settle for fighting him. I don't care if he's mad so long as he isn't ignoring me.

"Apologize?" Ellis runs his hand through his pale blond hair, letting the door swing close to shut out the noises from the hallway. With a quick flick of his finger, he snaps the lock, his brows pulling together with sudden focus. "What did you do, Devinee?"

"What do you mean, what did I do? I—" I cut off as I notice Ellis swaying slightly on his feet, his arm going out toward the wall for balance, though there is no change to the intensity of his eyes.

In anyone else, I'd make nothing of it. But Ellis isn't anyone. I hop off my perch, stalking up to him.

"What's going on?" I demand. The heat emanating from Ellis envelops me like a furnace. My hand closes around his hard biceps, and he flinches, his muscles coiled tight beneath my fingers. "Holy fucking shit," I whisper. "You're burning up."

"I'm fine." He shakes himself like a wet wolf. "I just need a minute to wash my face."

"You are not fine." Yanking him around to face me, I jerk his uniform shirt open. The buttons spring off and ping against mirror and walls. My gut is telling what I'm going to see even before I pull back the fabric to reveal angry red streaks snaking over his perfect skin and chiseled muscles beneath. My mouth dries. Dread and confirmation mix together. I know what I'm looking at. I've seen it before, in the cage when Ellis had iron shackles clamped around his wrists. "Iron poisoning. How the hell do you have iron poisoning?"

Ellis's back tightens, but he doesn't pull away. "The iron from the whip's tips got into my blood somehow. It doesn't matter. I'll heal. Without your involvement."

"Why are you being an asshole?"

A muscle clenches in Ellis's jaw, the many things he's not saying charging the air between us. "I have my reasons, and they are not your concern." His hand curls at his side, and he steps away, his Highland accent growing thick with anger. "Listen, Devinee. Ye make me vulnerable. Shite that shouldn't hurt me does hurt when yer around. So, if you want to help, get the hell away from me. And stay that way."

"You know what you are?" I shout right back into Ellis's face, my pulse pounding in my throat. "An injured wolf caught in a trap, snapping its teeth at anyone and everyone. And you know what? I don't give two fucks what you want right now." Before the male can realize what I'm about to do—before *I* fully realize—I press my palm over the mark on his chest.

2 4

Sam

The magic inside me wakens, like a key turning a lock to unleash the power within. Buzzing fills my blood, as if a million bees hum inside my veins. And then...

Pain so fierce that my howl echoes off the bathroom tile, my nerves scorching beneath the assault. My back is by far the worst, the skin and muscles sizzling with agony that spreads through me like wildfire. Breathing hurts. Moving hurts. Blood runs down my lip from where I've bitten it.

Through the haze of pain, I feel Ellis grip my shoulder to try to wrench my hand away from his chest. "Devinee! Stop. Let go."

I shake my head, sinking my magic's claws farther into him. Whatever I feel, it's only a fraction of what it's been doing to the male.

Somewhere, a door rattles, someone cursing colorfully on the other side.

Forcing a breath into my lungs, I struggle to get my

bearings, flexing the magic connecting Ellis and me. Feeling the iron that's the cause of all this, the poison that's coursing through his body. Once I've marked enough of the element, I grit my teeth and call it toward me.

Holy fuck. My back seems to open with hellfire that's spreading through my body, burning me from the inside. A keening sound fills the room, and I'm only vaguely aware that it's coming from me.

The rattling door gives way with a crash, followed by the sound of rushing footsteps. A familiar British voice demanding to know what the bloody hell is happening.

"I can't make her let go." Ellis's voice has a hint of panic as he pulls on my hand to try to get it away. But he can't. The claws of my magic have dug in hard. I can feel them. And I want them there no matter how much it hurts. For me, it's just pain. For Ellis, it's death.

"So I've gathered." Reese's face comes into view, though he looks like two versions of him separated slightly, as if I'm watching a 3D film without the glasses.

There *are* two version, I realize vaguely. One that I see through my eyes, the other through Ellis's.

"Do something, you bastard," Ellis snaps.

"I am." Reese's hand runs down along my back, cool and powerful.

I inhale his scent, his minty tang mixing with the caustic smell of chlorine used to clean this place. The room feels too hot. The air is too thick to breathe. "You'll have to break my hand to break the hold," I warn the males through clenched teeth. The iron that is burning through the life force of Ellis's magic seeps slowly into me. Progress, but still far to go. "And it won't work even then."

"I'm not going to break your hold, Samantha," Reese

promises, ignoring the fury that spills through Ellis into my blood. "But I will help."

I don't understand what he means until he rolls up his sleeve, the star-shaped scar on his forearm shiny beneath the overhead fluorescent lights.

"Samantha." Reese's voice is smooth and battle calm. Too calm considering what he says next. "I need to take a sip of your blood. That's the fastest way for me to know what's happening. Can you trust me to do that?"

I draw a shuddering breath, remember when Cassis sank his teeth into my neck to learn the truth about me. It was terrifying—but I didn't know him then. Didn't trust him. When Reese pricked my skin in the heat of passion, I liked it. Maybe it won't be so bad.

As if reading my mind, Reese says, "It will hurt more than before, Samantha. I'll have to bite much deeper. Are you ready?"

I nod once and feel his strong fingers move my head gently to one side, the callused thumbs running over my neck as my heart gallops.

"Don't be frightened," he says, as if it's something I have control over, as if the feeling of him next to my pulsing veins isn't sending a rush of terror through me. Without the heat of desire firing all my senses at once, it's just the bold facts: a predator about to sink his teeth into his natural prey. "I need to know what's happening, Samantha. If you are terrified, I'll get the fear, not the facts."

"You're about to bite me," I pant. "Not sure what you expect."

"Hold, Reesand." Ellis's tone takes on a note of command, and Reese crisply nods his consent. A heartbeat later, I feel the tendrils of Ellis's cool calm flow into me, easing the terror. Not fully, but enough to take the edge off. To let me know that I'm not alone.

I've never felt this connected to someone in my life, and despite the pain and fear, something deep inside wouldn't trade this for the world. To know that I can help. That someone wants to help me.

Ellis takes my face between his hands. "Look at me, Devinee." I do. I see the tiny specks of green in his golden eyes, his thick blond lashes, the shadows underneath that I wish I could wipe away. "Keep looking."

Reese's teeth puncture my neck, the immediate sting making me gasp. I hold Ellis's gaze as Reese pulls blood from my vein, his hands strong and supportive on my body. With the first pain of puncture gone, it burns, but not in an entirely unpleasant way. It's...strange. The warm slip of blood, the cool pressure of Reese's mouth a natural balm, almost numbing the area. The strange combination makes my heart pound, my breath come in short gasps.

A moment later, Reese lifts his mouth away and turns me toward him, his face serious and detached, though he rubs a small circle on the back of my shoulder. "Give me your other hand."

I try, but my palm only twitches.

He seems to get the idea and reaches for my hand himself. Before I have a chance to yelp, he makes a shallow cut across my palm with one nail, the tiny sting more unexpected than anything. His jaw set, Reese presses my hand to his forearm, my cut covering his scar.

My vision splits again, going haywire as images from three sets of eyes shift and overlap in a dizzying kaleidoscope of sensation. A sort of cool gel spills into my simmering veins, the addition simultaneously soothing and powerful. The buzzing inside my blood intensifies, which I think means I'm burning the iron more efficiently, but might just be a hallucination.

Wetness seeps through the hem of my skirt and covers my knees and shins where I'm now kneeling on the floor. Blinking, I see that the bathroom is now flooded with a thin layer of water, a burst pipe in the wall spilling onto the floor.

The back of Reese's hand wipes my face, and I realize a tear of pain has slipped over my cheek. Just one tear. The rest, apparently, the bathroom is weeping for me.

"Easy, witch," Reese is calm but unyielding. "Slow your breathing. Now."

I obey without thought, falling into a three-way connection. We stay like that for a short eternity, until the flow of iron from Ellis into me slows to a trickle and my magic pulls back the little claws it had sunk into the fae male.

Reese catches me as I sway, disoriented from the sudden loss of connection with Ellis. Instead of separating from me, Reese stays put, letting my hand keep drawing his strength until my muscles ease—and other things start flowing through the bond between us.

A female. Dark-haired and ethereal, laughing as rain pelts her skin. Eyes closed, she tips her face up to the clouds.

She is so real, so loved, that I want to reach out to her. But the moment I try, the mirage fades.

"Who was that?" I ask.

"My wife." Reese's words are curt. He reaches to pull my hand away from his forearm just as *something* jolts all three of us, as if a live wire has fallen onto the flooded floor.

Both males' grips on me tighten, confusion and readiness filling their faces as a clear soprano voice fills the air between us.

If you are listening to this message, then the time for vampire and fae and witch to join together has come. I do not expect you to forgive me my choices, nor do I apologize for them. But know that I never lied to you when I shared my dream—I only omitted that the time for it was not yet here. Everything I did, all the blood—yours and mine—was to ensure that the dream had a chance. And now the five of you can carry it forth. Your souls need each other, and the world needs you.

The voice stops, leaving nothing but a smell of burnt hickory behind.

I swallow. "Was that—"

"Yes," says Ellis, his voice penetrating through the darkening haze settling over me. "That was Sienna."

25

Sam

I open my eyes to blink at the harsh light, the smell of cleanliness and antiseptic filling my nose. Cool cotton presses against my skin, the crisp fabric stretching the length of my naked body. Yes. I'm definitely naked and lying on my stomach, a thin blanket covering me to the waist.

"Reesand," Ellis calls from the other side of the bed. "She's awake."

I want to turn toward him, but I ache too much for that. I remember nothing about how I got here. In fact, the last thing I have in my fuzz-filled mind is being in the flooded bathroom with Ellis and Reese and a shitload of magic.

A door swings opens on oiled hinges, and Reese's tall, powerful body fills my vision. Dressed in a pair of light-blue medical scrubs with his sleeves rolled up to show off corded forearms, the vamp has a severe look about him.

"Where am I?" My mouth feels thick, and I'm so thirsty. "Why am I here?"

"Infirmary. Because you acted first and thought never." Reese takes a thermometer off the counter and brushes it across my forehead, every movement executed with military precision. I wonder which Reese is in the room with me, the one who held me in the bathroom or the one who left without a word. "Thirty-seven point one. Slight elevation, but we are past the worst of it."

"If I had a thirty-seven-degree temperature, I'd be a block of ice," I mutter to him.

"Celsius, Samantha."

"Fuck you." I wince at my particular choice of epithet.

"You sure you're up for that just now?" Ellis says from my other side.

This time, I do manage to turn to look at him, just so I can glare. The male sits in a chair, looking pallid, but—except for the fatigue lining his face—much better than I last saw him. His pale blond hair hangs loose to his shoulders and is lightly damp as if he just showered. He wears slim jeans and a tight white V-neck that stretches across his pecs and shoulders, and somehow, this detail—Ellis wearing real clothes that don't look like they were pulled from a week-old laundry pile—comforts me more than anything else.

Running a hand through his already mussed blond hair, Ellis moves his chair closer to me, the concern in his eyes making me think I've been in the infirmary longer than I thought. Certainly long enough for someone—or someones—to have stripped me naked.

"You've been in and out of fever for two days," Ellis says, answering my unspoken question.

"Two days?" I echo. There's no way I've been out for two days.

"How are ye feeling?"

"Like I just sparred with you. Well, not quite *that* bad." I work my muscles, quickly realizing that my back hurts more than the rest of me. "My back feels like I have a bad sunburn."

"Good," Reese says, grabbing a clipboard with more force than necessary and scribbling something. "If you'd gotten past all the pain while unconscious, you'd be back at stupidity before the day is done."

The bite in Reese's voice stings. Wrapping the sheet around my chest, I push myself into a sitting position. Fuck it, I want clothes. It's hard enough to be around the warriors when I have my leather jacket and attitude intact, much harder when I'm sitting buck naked on bed. "I want to go back to my room."

Reese doesn't even look up from his notes. "Keep wanting."

Ellis sighs. "Don't mind Reesand. He's just upset you saved my life."

"I'm not sure I'm too keen on that either," I mutter, the memories of the asshole Ellis has been for the past month returning to me with a vengeance. But then I did get him whipped, so maybe we're even now. Either that or we have a pity-party kind of truth going on between us.

Reese slams his clipboard down on the counter, his blue eyes flashing. "I'm upset because you toyed with magic you neither understand or control. You could have gotten yourself killed, Samantha. Could have collapsed the building down on your head. Could have done a million other things that you don't even suspect, all because you're running around with a gun off safety and your finger on the bloody trigger."

"And he wasn't?" I point at Ellis, my blood rising along with Reese's voice. "Either you were too fucking blind to see that he was on the verge of collapse, or else you didn't give a damn. Which—"

"It was neither," Ellis cuts it. "Reesand knew the situation, but I made my own choices. Things didn't turn out the way I intended, but the decision wasn't the bloodsucker's, it was mine."

That just makes everything a hundred times worse. "Oh, so it's all right for him to make stupid choices," I snap at Reese, "but the moment I do something as reckless as try to save a life, you act like I'm a child with an M16?"

"Yes." Placing both hands on the edge of the bed, Reese looms over me, every line of his chiseled face tight with intensity. He's as furious as he's fucking gorgeous, and my thighs ache with the memory of how damn good he felt inside me. He scowls. "Ellis knew the risks. You had no bloody idea. That's the difference. And if you can't understand that, you are more of a child than I thought."

"What would you have had me do, Reese? Step over Ellis's corpse and go wash up?"

"You were supposed to get me," says Reese. "Do things in a controlled way."

"You mean *your* controlled way, don't you?" I shoot back, and I wonder if he knows I'm not talking about magic anymore. "Though for all I know, you'd scurried off somewhere again. It's not as if you bothered to give anyone a heads-up last time."

Reese's lips pull back, but he says nothing, the pair of us staring at each other until he turns and walks away—which seems to be the damn vampire's signature move. I stare at the door long after it closes. "If you have something to say about what I should or shouldn't have done, Ellis, please keep it to yourself."

"You frightened him, Devinee," Ellis says, the words rolling off him casually. "You frightened both of us. Not that I'm not grateful, mind ye. But I still have an itch to prod you with something just to make sure ye are really awake."

"Let me punch you in the nose, and you can have a full fucking reminder," I say, my strength draining from me. Maybe I was overly optimistic about getting out of the infirmary right away. "Does this mean you don't hate me anymore?" I ask Ellis as I settle back down on the bed.

"Oh, I still despise you," he assures me. "But it's a friendly kind of despise." Stepping closer to me, he adjusts my blankets, his fingers lingering on my hair. "We need to talk, Devinee. When you're feeling better. We need to talk."

26

Sam

"Please take a seat." Victor smiles—an incredible rendition of kind, fatherly concern—and gestures to an armchair before his huge cherrywood desk. The entire office looks like something that was transposed from a different century. Heavy wood paneling. Leather chairs. Even the lamps have been shaped like old-fashioned candle lanterns while still getting the most out of electricity. Thick velvet curtains are pulled over the windows, blocking out the bright morning light.

Victor leans forward, clasping his hands together on his desk so his sapphire cuff links clink the wood lightly. "I understand that you were recently released from the infirmary. How are you feeling, Samantha?"

Like a magical washing machine ran me through its heavy soil cycle. "Quite well, thank you, sir," I answer smoothly.

I wonder just how much he knows. How much Reese told

him. If Reese speaks to Victor as much as he's spoken to me the past couple of days, probably very little. Since I first woke up two days ago, there's been a quiet heaviness saturating the air between Ellis, Reese, and me, the knowledge of a conversation to come hanging over all of us. I know Cassis and Asher stopped in as well, but I was mostly asleep. Or faked being asleep.

Yes, I can be a coward sometimes, but I'm not sure what to say to any of them. Not after what Sienna's voice said in those final moments I was conscious. I'd thought the words a dream at first, but I'm more and more convinced they were real. That Ellis and Reese heard them as well.

But before I can deal with Reese and Ellis, I have to deal with Victor.

I sit in the chair opposite his desk, resisting the urge to straighten my uniform. My white blouse and blue plaid skirt already mark me as inferior to the grand count without me letting my body language bring attention to it. Or to the fact that Victor is making me nervous. Hell, if I don't fool him, maybe I can at least fool myself. Faking it was one of the best skills I learned in the foster homes.

The other thing I learned was to let the other guy speak first. Information is power.

Silence trickles through the room for a moment before Victor flips open a file on his desk, though I'm willing to bet anything the reference is just for show.

"I understand your recent illness came upon you after you healed Ellis, who'd been concealing a bout of iron poisoning?" Victor says. "Is that right?"

"I'm not sure exactly what I did," I answer. "I was more acting on instinct than anything. But I'm glad it all turned out for the best."

"I am not sure the plumbing would agree." A small smile tugs the corner of Victor's mouth.

"No, probably not, sir." I don't add that Reese would not agree either.

Victor sighs, leaning back in his chair and tenting his fingers. "I do regret that things turned out the way they did. Ellis is...prideful. He is here on orders from an overbearing father who thought making an ancient warrior into a first-year cadet was a good means of discipline. If I'd been here at the time, I'd never have allowed it. Such a childish move might appease King Bryant's personal taste, but for the rest of the cadets—such as yourself—its effects have ranged from disruptive to downright dangerous." Victor shakes his head ruefully. "There are a great many choices I would have made otherwise had I all the information at hand."

The last part of that is clearly a bait, though I can't for the life of me figure out what he's leading me toward. Still, I walk through the door that he's opened. Information is information, and I can't afford to scoff at it just because it happens to come from Victor's lips. I certainly don't scoff at the runes he shows me.

"What information would have led you to a different decision, sir?" I ask.

"Well, knowing Ellis's medical situation, for starters. The male didn't just have a severe case of iron poisoning—he kept it from everyone."

Bullshit. Reese knew. Did he not tell Victor, or is Victor lying? Keeping the thoughts to myself, I nod along sympathetically, encouraging the male to continue.

"If I'd been aware of the severity of the situation, I'd have insisted Ellis return to Talon to recuperate. The care he'd have received there, with fae healers, would have been more effective than anything we could do here. Well, nearly anything." He gives me another wry smile. "Plus, fae have their full magic in Talon, which would certainly have helped Ellis battle the iron poisoning. Do you think…" Victor's face changes, his sharp features tightening in concern, and he leans toward me. "I hate asking this question, but I feel it would be irresponsible not to. Samantha, do you think Ellis may have stayed here on purpose? As a test to see if your powers were capable of countering iron?"

"I don't see why he would care, sir," I say. "Ellis was whipped for helping me, and he's made no secret of wanting nothing to do with me since." The last forty-eight hours notwithstanding.

"Don't be naïve, Samantha," Victor says harshly. "It doesn't become you. If Ellis truly wanted nothing to do with you, he'd have left. I'd have helped him negotiate with his father and the council. No, I think it is safe to say that Ellis remained here for a reason. A witch being able to mitigate the effects of iron in the mortal world—that's a very powerful tool. Surely you see the value of that?"

I don't know what to say to that, except that I don't think Ellis is manipulating me. Sienna is taking care of that part.

Victor sighs. "I want you to be very careful, Samantha. It was Ellis and his father who led to your getting to Talonswood —right when Asher was de facto in charge. Neither Asher nor the rest of the fae seem to have an interest in you learning to control your powers, though if my theory is correct, they are curious to explore the extent to which those powers reach. I can't tell you why or what this might mean, but I wanted you to be aware."

"Yes, sir," I say uncomfortably. Though my neck prickles with unease, I can't refute any separate part of what Victor said—but I guess that's his superpower. He speaks in facts while somehow shedding doubt on the truth. "I'll be aware."

"Very good. That is all I ask." Victor's face relaxes. "Now then, speaking of *control,* how are things going with the rune? Once you feel comfortable with the small locks, I'd like to introduce slightly larger objects."

27

Reese

Reese had been less nervous than this in Afghanistan, where Jack had sent him to retrieve a kid from a nest of asshole vamps who'd snatched the boy from his diplomat parents. Sitting with Ellis and Samantha in the main room of his and Asher's suite, Reese could barely keep himself still. Finally giving up, he stood and walked over to the door, snapping the lock into place.

They wouldn't be interrupted now, at least. Whether that was good or bad, he wasn't sure. He didn't like the sensations Samantha's mere presence sparked in his body, liked even less the ones she sent sweeping through his soul. And yet the week he'd been away had been one of the worst since Sienna. Thinking had been hard. Staying still near impossible. And with every passing day, he'd felt like he was getting physically ill. Fevers were not exactly a common occurrence for vampires, yet his temperature had risen. By the time he'd gotten the kid safe, he didn't even stay long enough for Jack to make him another offer.

He got on a plane and came to Talonswood. And then went in to see the witch in the middle of a bloody test, without even bothering to change first, and she'd been sitting there in that pert little skirt that made his cock twitch, and his head had finally stopped throbbing, and his lungs had opened fully, like breaking the surface of a deep, deep lake.

There was nothing normal about that.

And given what Sienna's voice had said in the bathroom, it *wasn't* normal.

Which meant that Ellis was right. The three of them had to talk. Fuck it, the five of them had to talk, but bringing Cassis and Asher into this just now would be like throwing gasoline on a fire. Especially since Reese hadn't wanted additional company when Samantha inevitably told him how little he mattered. That he was a good fuck and that was that.

Not only was Reese connected with a witch, he was connected with a witch he didn't trust. Not when it came to what she could do to him.

"So, where do we start?" Samantha asked, pulling her leather jacket around her. She wore that jacket as a piece of armor, and Reese wondered whether she knew how the worn leather molded around her full breasts, how when he looked at her bare legs under her school skirt, he could think of nothing but wrapping them around his waist.

Fuck.

"With whiskey." Getting up, Ellis walked over to the liquor shelf and helped himself to three glasses, filling them all with the amber liquid.

Reese hesitated a moment before accepting his. Taking something from Ellis's hand was too much of a truce flag—

and after the prick had fled to Talon, right back to the king against whom they'd all fought, Reese wasn't sure he wanted a truce. Finally taking the glass and a long swig of alcohol, Reese turned to Samantha—and cut right to the chase. "I want to know what the hell happened after we had sex."

Ellis leaned back in his seat, grinning like an idiot. "Well, if I knew this was going to be the topic of conversation, I'd have pressed for us to chat earlier. Can you back up? I want details, Devinee. How much better am I than the bloodsucker?"

The witch's face turned pink, and Reese swore he scented her arousal, a mere brush of what had flooded out of her when he'd taken charge of her in bed—or what passed for one.

Ellis's nostrils flared, taking in the same scent Reese just did, but coming to an additional conclusion. "The witch is embarrassed."

Sam wheeled on Ellis, her fists tightening. "If you're so eager to talk, you want to tell me why you've been an asshole to me ever since…" She cuts off. "Never mind. I don't need an explanation. I got you whipped. You hated me. I healed you. Now you have some sort of pity friendship going. And I'm tired of it. Pick a mood and stick to it."

Reese raised a brow and swallowed a comment about pots and kettles.

Ellis's hand froze with the whiskey glass halfway to his lips. "Bloody hell, Dev, you being responsible for my whipping is the stupidest thing I've ever heard. It's that—that had nothing to do with anything."

"Then what sparked the hate, exactly?" Samantha demanded.

"Nothing." Ellis rubbed his face. "I didn't like pushing you away, Devinee. I—"

"If the next words out of your mouth are even related to

'it's not you, it's me,' or 'I just don't think I'm in a position to provide you with what you deserve,' please do us both a favor and shove them up your ass," Sam said. Her body had tightened in on itself as if bracing for a blow, and she was swallowing rapidly. "I've been tossed away enough to know how the story goes. I heard enough of that bullshit by age six to stop believing it."

Bloody hell. Reese had understood Ellis's reasons for keeping Samantha in the dark, but when she put it that way...

Before he could finish the thought, Ellis jumped out of his chair and prowled over to Samantha, covering her mouth with his. The girl gasped lightly as the wolf fae parted her lips predatorily before angling her head and sweeping his tongue into her mouth in a way that made Reese's rare heartbeat pound against his chest.

Hades take him, but the witch's body yielded to Ellis's demand with such succulent intensity that Reese knew she was already wet. She clung to Ellis's neck, tiny whimpers caught in her throat, and Reese could imagine what he'd feel if he slid his hand between her thighs at just this moment. His cock could imagine it too, waking and pressing against his pants.

Sam panted as Ellis pulled away, her full lower lip wet and tempting. Taking the witch's face in his hands, Ellis captured her gaze with his, his own pants bulging as prominently as Reese's.

"That was not a thank-you kiss." Ellis sounded raspy. "In case you were wondering."

"What was it?" Sam whispered.

"The truth," Reese said quietly, and Ellis didn't even glare.

Sam's face flushed pink again, and Reese wondered whether she'd forgotten he was there altogether until he'd spoken.

"I want you, Devinee," Ellis told Sam, his hands flattening

on her cheeks. Reese took this as his cue to leave the room as quickly as his feet would carry him, lest he became unable to resist claiming a piece of the witch himself.

"Don't think you're leaving, bloodsucker." Ellis's voice hit Reese in the back just as he was a step away from the door.

"I didn't know you required direction on what to do next," Reese said.

"Don't you want to join in?" Ellis asked, the bastard clearly enjoying the one-upsmanship. Reese would kill him. Slowly. But not now.

"You aren't my type, Ellis," Reese said.

"No, but Devinee wants you too."

Funny. Reese reached for the door.

"Wait." This time, it was Samantha's voice, her footsteps coming up to him. Her fingers brushing his shoulder in a way that made his whole world narrow down to that soft touch. Her breath hitched, her sweet citrusy smell halting Reese in place no matter how much his brain screamed at him to keep walking. To *run*. She cleared her throat. "I owe you an explanation too."

Reese kept staring at the door. It had been a long time since he was afraid, but he was now. And it was better to make the cut himself. "You don't owe me anything. I apologize for taking advantage of the moment. We were—emotional and drunk on sensation. One-night stands have been a standard for me for some time, but I should have known better than to put you into that position."

Instead of softening, Sam's muscles tightened, her hand digging into Reese's shoulder. The smell of fury wafted from her, tickling his nose. "So that's all it was? I was just a one-night stand to you?"

"I was a one-night stand to *you*." Reese twisted around, shaking off Sam's hand. "Don't rewrite history. I apologize for not having stopped it, apologize that you didn't enjoy yourself. You should have told me to stop. Did you imagine I wouldn't have?"

"I didn't want to tell you to stop," Sam blurted. "That's the fucking problem."

Reese stared. "You feared saying no?"

"No, God damn you, I didn't." Color rose so high on Sam's face that for a moment, Reese wondered if the witch was getting a fever. She was certainly making as much sense as someone in the midst of delirium. "I didn't say stop because *I didn't want you to stop*. Don't you understand?"

"I think she means you failed to satisfy her," Ellis put in helpfully.

Samantha threw him a glare.

With a short growl, Reese gripped Sam's chin between his thumb and forefinger, forcing the witch to meet his eyes. And, Hades take him, her breath hitched with arousal so quickly, it made his cock ache. He held her there, watching as her pupils dilated, the small soft spot on the side of her neck vibrating with a quickening pulse. It was all he could do to keep from taking her mouth right then and there, but there was something else he needed to work out first. And he would stand there until hell froze over if he had to.

"Explain," Reese ordered.

Samantha gasped lightly, her arousal spiking, her body yielding beautifully in his grip. "I…" She swallowed, her voice changing. "Weren't you leaving?"

"I was," Reese confirmed. "But now I'm not."

"Well, change your fucking mind again!"

"No."

"You enjoyed taking Reesand, Dev." Ellis stepped up to them, arms crossed over his wide chest, his body blocking

Sam's path to the door. "Why are you so intent on convincing everyone that you didn't?"

"Because I shouldn't have enjoyed it," Samantha mumbled.

"Why is that?" said Reese, not yielding an inch of ground. "Because I'm a vampire?"

"What? No!" Sam shut her eyes tightly. "I'm... I don't like that I liked it."

"Look at me," ordered Reese, certain that he'd be obeyed. And he was. In fact, if he was smelling right, moisture was dripping from Sam's sex down the inside of her thighs as he held her. "Why shouldn't you enjoy sex?"

"I should enjoy...*normal* sex," Samantha blurted finally, the desperation in her tone tugging at Reese's heart. "Not *that* sex. What we did—letting you... It was wrong. I'm not the kind of person who enjoys... I don't want to be that person."

"Hades take me, Samantha," said Reese, the realization finally, *finally* dawning on him. "Are you seriously telling me that you think what you enjoy sexually is some sort of commentary on who you are as a person?"

"Not that I want to give Cassis credit," Ellis said, stepping up behind Sam so she was boxed in between them, "but the bastard always said Talonswood Reform could do with some sex education."

28

Sam

My face flames so much that I can't even find my words. Wrong. Everything about this conversation is so, so wrong. Worse still, Reese's brilliant blue eyes have a hint of gentle amusement dancing inside them, the lightness clashing with an equal dose of panty-soaking intensity.

"I enjoy taking females from behind," he says, each word seemingly calculated to go straight to my clit. "I don't think that makes me a dog. Nor do I think that your enjoying me taking charge of you in bed means you'd like for me to do so in real life."

"Can we please move on to something else now?" I say, trying to focus on anything except the image Reese just planted in my head. "A discussion of spiders would be good. Or snakes."

Reese wraps his hand in my hair and pulls my head back to look at me from above, the slight prickling in my scalp doing nothing to soothe the ache in my thighs. His dark eyes grip mine, his nostrils flaring. "I am a vampire," he says, his voice low. "A predator. It is part of who I am. If you would like me to keep myself in check sexually, I will. But don't let human myths destroy your pleasures, Samantha. Your body is your own."

I bite my lip, wanting more of him. Wanting Ellis. Wanting to stop being afraid of what my body is screaming at me to do. "What if I don't know what I like?" I whisper.

Behind me, Ellis's warm hands slide along my arms and waist, stopping right at the curve of my hip. "Then I think it will be our pleasure to find that out," he purrs into my ear. "In my experience, such questions are too important to leave to chance."

It takes me a moment to realize what he's suggesting, to see that Reese is moving even closer to me, angling my head to nibble his way from my jaw to my earlobe. Apparently, my orgasms are the one and only thing in this universe on which Ellis and Reese agree.

"No strings attached," Reese whispers into my ear. "Other than trust. For this one hour. Can you trust us?"

I look between them, my voice breathless. "You want to—"

"How else will you know who is better?" Ellis points out with a raised brow, his hand sliding steadily up the inside of my thigh, closer and closer to the throbbing wetness I know he'll find there.

"Don't you two hate each other?" I say. My one last desperate protest falls out of me in a breathy tumble as the two hot-as-hell males bracket me on either size, my body a tuned violin begging to be played with, whether or not my mind thinks it's a good idea.

"Very much so." Ellis runs a finger along my cheekbone, "I'm planning on pleasuring you, not the bloodsucker."

Reese snorts as Ellis's hand moves that last inch up my skirt, the tip of one finger sliding into the crotch of my panties and making me stand up on my toes. As I gasp, something passes between the two males, and, a heartbeat later, Ellis sits himself on the couch and pulls me onto his lap. Crouching in front, Reese reaches beneath my skirt and pulls my underwear clean off.

Cool air brushes my sex, but before I can do anything, Ellis has his hands firmly on the insides of my thighs. He pushes my legs apart, strong fingers stroking between my slippery folds, circling my entrance without ever going inside. Unable to help it, I moan and relax my legs farther apart, resting my head on Ellis's shoulder. I don't even care what Reese can see right now.

Not that it would matter if I did. Ellis nips my earlobe lightly before hooking one leg around mine so that I'm trapped. Exposed. And oh so very hot. My heart quickens, and it's only partially because Ellis has just traced the hood of my clit.

Licking his lips, Reese pulls off my jacket and shirt and bra, until the little blue skirt is all I have on. In the late afternoon shadows, my nipples perk in the cool air. My breasts tremble with each of my heaving breaths. Without warning, Reese pulls one nipple into his cool mouth and flicks it with his tongue, making me gasp. Ellis's hand tightens around my waist, his other pressing my sex with a competent possessiveness that would have me squirming if he wasn't holding me quite so tightly.

Grabbing my shirt, Reese tears a wide swatch of fabric from it and approaches me. "Stop thinking," he whispers, his words low and commanding as he lays the cloth over my eyes and deftly ties it around the back of my head.

I freeze, my breaths coming quick and tight as my sight

disappears. My heart races, the knowledge that I can't see what's happening rushing through me to wake all my other senses. The rough cloth of Ellis's jeans beneath my bare ass, the fae's foresty scent mixing with the vamp's tangy one. A clock somewhere tick-tick-ticks the seconds away.

Ellis shifts to slide his warm palms over my aching breasts, rubbing my nipples in small circles, then kneading my breasts deeply. I arch my back with a whimper, pressing my chest harder into his hands. Now a second set of hands caresses my arms.

Reese. Telling me where he is without speaking. My heart slows a bit, my breathing deepening. His hands slide up my bare legs agonizingly slowly, from my splayed-open knees to my inner thighs.

Without warning, he flicks his finger right over my clit, and I squirm, whatever calm I just earned disappearing into a deep, deep need. More. I want more.

I gasp, opening my mouth to— "Do not move," Reese orders in that voice from the gym, the one that makes me go stock-still, even as a new wave of arousal races through my quivering body. Fuck. Three words. The vamp has made me even needier and wetter with three little words.

Slipping farther between my thighs, one callused hand slides through my moist folds, up and down, up and down, making wet sounds in the silent room. With deft, confident strokes, he moves closer and closer to my clit, never touching it.

A sound I don't recognize escapes my body, a long, breathless cry as he teases my sensitive lips, thrusts a finger shallowly into my channel, again. Then two fingers, pistoning deeply, rhythmically, almost enough to—

But then he pulls out just as quickly, leaving me achingly empty. I groan and protest with my hips, turning my forehead into Ellis's hot neck. But the fae's legs only tighten around mine, holding me pinned as Reese continues to work his way along my sex. Tracing the hood of my engorged clit, flicking on either side with short teasing motions that become more impossible to endure with every heartbeat.

Ellis circles my nipples with his fingertips now, twisting them lightly to the rhythm of Reese's flicks.

My whole body trembles and bucks, the intensity of the sensation consuming my consciousness. My need goes higher and higher, taking over the world, making me writhe against Ellis's hands and cry desperately for release.

Reese presses two fingers right against my clit and makes tiny, tight circles, and I plummet into an orgasmic free fall. I scream as my channel clenches in pleasure over and over, the shocks coming one after another.

I'm melted, boneless, against Ellis.

But the males aren't done.

With a blindfold in place, I don't realize what's about to happen until I'm suddenly being lifted off Ellis's lap and laid on my back on the rug. I try to sit up on instinct, but hard hands grip my thighs and shoulders at once. Push me down. Holding me there as a new rush of need simmers in my blood.

And then...nothing. A pause. I draw a ragged breath, straining to make out the sounds for any clues of what's happening around me.

"I think I want your attention a little more focused," Reese's British voice informs me, his callused hands pushing my thighs apart so wide that I feel the cool air brush the steaming inside of my sex and butt. He releases me, but instead of appeasing my need, the sudden freedom is absurdly disappointing—right up until I feel Reese's finger trace the rim of my anus.

My heart stops. All my muscles tighten at once as my heart pounds my ribs. "N—"

"Consider it a warning," Reese tells me, his voice powerful and low and so intense, it makes moisture drip down my ass and pool beneath me on the rug. "I would suggest you keep very, very still. No matter what I do."

The ominous words, which should send any normal being sprinting straight for the door, instead turn up the heat on my fucked-up thermostat. I stop moving at once and whimper as his hands grip the insides of my thighs tightly and—

I gasp, barely keeping my hips on the floor as Reese's tongue parts my folds, lapping up and gathering moisture. Long, slow strokes of his tongue up through my folds, then quick flicks of my clit. Like a predator enjoying his dessert. Everything inside me tightens with the desire to raise my hips, to do *something* to create more of that delicious friction, to speed my body toward climax.

Yet just when I'm ready to give in and buck my hips, Reese brushes that warning finger against my back hole again.

I rein in all thought of moving at once. And nearly come just from that yielding alone.

With all my attention on Reese's tongue and on trying to keep still, I almost forget about Ellis—who, until now, has had his hands resting tamely on my shoulders. Now, those hands slide down to cup my aching breasts.

Ellis rolls my right nipple between his thumb and forefinger, and I whimper as it puckers beneath his hold. He squeezes just a bit harder, taking me to an edge of pain that is not pain at all. I pant, the effort of holding myself still over Reese's lapping, sucking mouth, against Ellis's fingers arousing my nipples to hard, hard points.

Zings of electricity jolt through me, waking my clit and

making everything from my thighs to my toes tighten beneath the assault.

I tremble as Reese's tongue continues to explore my sex, tormenting the hood with merciless flick flick flicks. Each touch sends new waves of desire through me, bringing me up to climax one rung at a time. And just when I think I have no other place to go, when the orgasm is within a millimeter's reach, the bastard pulls back. I moan in frustration and try to bring my knees closer together, preparing for whatever's coming next.

A palm connects loudly with my ass, making me yelp.

"Obey, Samantha," Reese growls over me.

He slaps my other cheek, harder. Again. I pant loudly, the slaps vibrating directly to my clit, nearly pushing me over the edge.

Ellis's mouth closes over my puckered nipple just as Reese plunges his finger into my tightening channel, everything about it magnified by my blindfold. Ellis's mouth, hot and powerful as it suckles my breasts. My chest full and achy. Reese's finger filling my sex in promise of bigger things to come.

Holy hell. I lick my lips, imagining what it might feel like to take one of the males into my mouth. To feel the thick velvety cock against my tongue, to make them ache with pleasure the way they torment me.

"She's thinking again," Ellis points out, lifting his head from my nipple and blowing on the sensitive flesh.

"Hmm," Reese agrees. "There will be punishment for that."

The vamp's words roll over my skin, the menacing promise in them making my whole body scream with need.

Reese plunges another finger inside me, pumping back and

forth, back and forth, until I'm whimpering, mewling like a helpless needy kitten.

Then he pulls out. Parts my ass cheeks.

A rush off anxiety floods me, my ass wiggling in an attempt to escape the unyielding hold as a finger traces my rim insistently, and this time—this time, it is no longer a threat. It's a promise.

"Punishment," he growls, and slips his finger inside.

A small burn as he passes the sensitive rim of muscle gives way to molten heat that floods my body. My breath halts, my sex clenching over and over. The slick finger inside my ass moves, Reese pushing in and out, in and out, in the most intimate and intrusive way. So certain. So insistent. Never allowing me to escape each and every moment of the intense sensation.

I draw a shuddering breath.

And then, with his finger still inside my tight hole, he flicks his tongue right over my apex and sends me headlong over the edge again.

I scream as I come, and Ellis covers my mouth with his, swallowing all my moans while my body spasms uncontrollably. Waves of pleasure rush through my core, gripping the backs of my thighs, my sex, my toes. My hands curl on the carpet, looking for purchase, for anything to ground me as Reese's fingers start moving in and out again and again and again.

The second orgasm hits me on the heels of the first, the two sets of spasms crashing into each other like a tsunami of pure pleasure. So intense, it's painful. All-consuming. My heart races, my hands clawing the carpet, my hips bucking and undulating against Reese's and Ellis's dual unyielding holds. They don't let go. Don't let me up. And my treacherous body only takes the restraint as spice that intensifies each sensation.

I'm panting and whimpering as the last waves of my orgasm finally shudder to a stop, my body feeling too heavy and melted and exhausted to be in the here and now.

For a few moments, nothing happens, both males withdrawing from me, and I imagine what I must look like to them, splayed half-naked on the rug like a rag doll. Just when I'm about to break out of the position, a minty scent washes over me, and I'm lifted again, held against a cool bare chest. I feel the lightest brush of fangs over my neck, my pulse pounding in response.

"Do you think the little witch has learned her lesson?" the vamp growls, his chest vibrating against me.

Stripping away the skirt that's proving more hindrance than cover now, he carries me somewhere—it feels like the couch—and sits, settling me down so I'm kneeling over his lap, facing away from him. My legs are spread wide over his, every inch of me exposed to their eyes. Their hands.

I hear a rustling, a warm presence stepping in front of me. "What shall we do with you now?" Ellis whispers into my ear, his words tickling and warm.

"I want to…" I can't make myself speak the words. Can't tell him how much I want to take him into my mouth. It's too—

"What do you want to do?" Ellis whispers, brushing his lips over my ear. "You'll have to speak up."

Right. *Stop thinking, Devinee.* They're not going to let up until I let my body take over, until I take what I want from them.

"I want to taste you," I say finally, my words so low, they're almost inaudible even to me. But I know he heard them loud and clear.

A cool hand slides down my spine, under my ass, and between the folds of my sex, teasing my entrance from behind. "Very good, Samantha. You'll get a reward for that," Reese says, and I feel my juices drench his hand. "Lean forward," he orders, and fuck if that voice doesn't nearly make me come a fourth time.

I obey at once, bracing my hands on his muscular thighs, my heavy breasts swaying beneath me.

"Keep your mouth open," he demands.

I freeze. Do as I'm told. Not daring to hope.

A moment later, the head of Ellis's amazing, warm cock presses between my lips.

Oh holy hell. YES. I moan and take him into my mouth hungrily, sucking the thick viscous saltiness. I run my tongue over the velvety skin that is stretched taut. I want so much more.

Reese grips my hips, lifting me, and I feel his rock-hard cock at my entrance. And then he pulls me down and thrusts up at once, filling my channel so suddenly, I scream around Ellis's cock. The two males thrust together the next time, giving me no quarter. I tilt forward with the force, but Reese digs his fingers into my hips, pulling me back hard against him.

The males find their rhythm, thrusting in counterpoint to each other. In and out, in and out, Ellis's cock alive and pulsing in my mouth. The fae male's warmth is an utter contrast to the coolness of the vampire's cock on the other end. Hot and cold. In and out. Full and throbbing and inescapable and everywhere.

I use my own legs to help, riding Reese's cock with my hips, my forward tilt making my clit rub against his hardness with every stroke.

The rhythmic pounding fills the room, the sounds of my suckling mixing with the wet slap of Reese's skin against mine. Ellis breathes heavily above me, pressing harder into my mouth. Snaking his hand beneath me, the vamp teases my clit right in its engorged center.

I gasp, sucking on Ellis so hard that his thickness hits the back of my throat just as a shattering orgasm cascades through my body. My channel spasms around Reese's cock over and over, my cries bouncing off the walls. If I thought the first three climaxes had wrecked my body, this one launches me off a new height, all my muscles contracting at once. A moment later, thick liquid slides down my throat, just as Reese's cock spills warmth into me, and I can do nothing to stop yet another tsunami of pleasure from hitting me so hard that I see stars and scream.

29

Sam

"You've no intention of storming out of the room, right?" Reese asks, watching me cautiously over his whiskey, one dark brow lifted.

Both males lounge near me on the leather furniture. And by lounge, I mean Ellis has shifted into his wolf form and now takes up most of the couch, his fluffy white head squarely in my lap. I'm wearing one of Reese's long shirts, a warm satisfied glow making my limbs heavy—and I know it's not just from the hundred-year-old whiskey I'm sipping.

I shake my head. "Are you itching to run off and kill someone in the Middle East?"

Reese's pause is too long for comfort, and I push Ellis's wolf off my lap to lean forward and frown at the vamp. The wolf whines unhappily, but shifts back into fae form, Ellis crossing his arms over his chest as he takes in the silence. His hair has dried into wild blond strands, which he takes the time now to tie back into a knot.

"What did I miss?" he asks.

"Samantha wanted to know if I had the intention of going to a different continent," says Reese, his voice heavy with meaning that Ellis seems to understand better than I do.

A chill settles over me, and I place my glass down on the coffee table with deliberate slowness. Studying the vamp's beautiful face, I find the muscle on the side of his jaw tight with the same tension that grips his shoulders, his blue eyes very carefully neutral. My stomach clenches into a heavy ice cold knot. "You want to leave."

"I'm not sure that *want* figures into the equation," Reese says quietly.

I force my clenched fists open, ordering my fucking body to stop feeling. "You need to leave."

Reese shakes his head.

"The bloodsucker isn't sure he *can* leave," Ellis says, blissfully cutting to the chase. "It's possible that Sienna did something to us." Reaching over to me, he uncurls my fingers to reveal the star-shaped scar.

The witch's words in the bathroom. The ones I've been going back and forth on, wondering if they were a delusion-filled dream. "Something like what?"

Reese taps his finger on his whiskey glass. "When you were in the infirmary, I looked through your medical records. You'd stopped in for some medicine while I was gone."

I nod, struggling to follow the change in direction. "I had a bit of a fever, nothing huge."

"And is that common for you?" Reese asks.

"No, but it's hardly uncommon."

"It is uncommon when you are a vampire," says Reese. "And I had it too."

"You think Sienna had something to do with it?" I ask. "The voice in the bathroom—"

"So you do remember." Ellis cocks a brow, and I have the decency to blush. "We think she did something, but we don't know what exactly. For whatever reason, physical distance between you and Reesand created a problem. Would the same be true if it were me who left? Or Asher? Or did sex have something to do with triggering it? We have no idea."

I pinch the bridge of my nose, not sure what I'm supposed to do with this information. "What does any of this have to do with you being an asshole to me?" I ask, returning to familiar —if not more comfortable—ground.

"I thought Sienna pushed us together," Ellis says, capturing my eyes with his golden gaze. "And I wanted—I want you to make your own choices, not play out a game Sienna's spells may have carved into us. No matter how badly I long for you, if you never want to repeat what we did today, then we will not."

Each of the male's words hits an aching spot in my heart, which pounds a steady, desperate beat against my chest. My breath quickens as I lean toward him, this male who's made me cry. Who came when I called. Who protected my choices. My power.

I press my mouth against his, and he hesitates only a moment before returning the kiss. Deep, powerful, and so claiming that my magic wakens with a buzz inside me, my soul purring its content.

Reese clears his throat, and Ellis lifts a hand from my cheek to flip the vampire off.

I laugh, pressing my head into the male's muscled chest as I turn to take in Reese—and the rest of reality crashes into our perfect moment. "So we're all stuck together now?" I ask. "What about Asher and Cassis? Are they...stuck with me too?"

Reese raises one powerful shoulder, his face sober. "We do

not know the nature of the bond Sienna wove, but I agree with Ellis—whatever this thing between us may mean for magic, or proximity or lust, our feelings are our own." Reaching out with one hand, he traces his thumb over my cheekbone.

I swallow, nodding at his words. Now that my mind is no longer in the gutter, I see the vulnerable male Cassis warned me about, the one who is as utterly terrified of getting hurt as I am. Leaning toward him, I kiss the vampire's cool cheek. "Then we'll all take things day by day."

30

Ellis

*E*llis stuck his hands into his pockets and watched Asher swear at his computer for a good ten minutes before finally shutting the laptop with a disgruntled snap. Despite the sunlight streaming into the male's office, the room had an aura of frustration jamming every bit of space between the various military memorabilia Asher had gathered over the centuries.

"If anything you are about to say includes the words *fight, brawl, disruption, destruction,* or *witch,* please shove yourself down the nearest well and save me the trouble," said Asher.

Grabbing a chair, Ellis turned it around and straddled it. "You are the one who wanted this bloody job."

"That was before one overbred Romanian vampire and an equally frustrating witch managed to take everything apart bit by bloody bit."

A growl rose deep in Ellis's chest, and Asher raised his chin, meeting his glare head-on.

"Don't you fucking start, brother. You want to be protective of your mate, take her to Talon. So long as you're both here, I want to hear nothing of it." Asher rubbed the heel of his hand over his eyes, fatigue lining his face.

"Then would this be a poor time to tell you that it's *possible* you will never be able to get any significant physical distance between yourself and Devinee?" Ellis inquired lightly. He waited until Asher released another impressive string of obscenities before filling him in on what happened when Reese went away. "Sienna wanted to ensure that the five of us would continue fighting for the dream, so it's not that far a leap to imagine she'd try to stop us from getting too far apart."

"Sienna was a deranged lunatic," Asher said flatly. "You assembled the horsemen in the middle of the fae-vamp wars to fight for peace between species. There is no war now, bar the fistfights between demis that Sam seems to start and Victor does nothing to discourage. Sienna was wrong. And I don't just mean what she did to us, but I mean about everything. From what was needed then to what might be needed in the future."

Ellis tapped his finger on the back of the chair. Asher had a mind for strategy, and what he said made sense. To a point. "What about our mating? However it happened, Devinee *is* my mate, Asher. She may be yours too."

"She isn't," Asher said with more force than necessary. "My body lusts after her as if I were an adolescent cub, but that's all it is. Oh, I wouldn't put it past Sienna to have *tried* to create a connection, but the only place I feel it is in my cock—and no one has died of a hard-on yet. Plus, Reese's little proximity problem didn't happen until after he bedded the witch. So I'll take that as a warning to the wise, as if I needed one."

"But—"

Asher held up a silencing hand. "Meanwhile, Victor is

claiming there's been an increase in gateway activity into Talon—any idea what that's about?"

Ellis blinked at the change of topic, shaking his head. Back to business. "None at all. But how does Victor know one way or the other what's happening at the gateway? Vamps aren't exactly welcome there anywhere near the building."

"Not unless they are leading a Talonswood Reform education field trip," Asher said dryly. "Which he did. Packed up a dozen cadets and took them sightseeing." He sighed, his voice changing to something softer. "Do you miss it, Ellis? Talon, I mean."

Ellis let out a long breath. His return to Talon, to the jackass who sat on the Talon throne, had been the spark of the other horsemen's hatred for him. But by the time Sienna was done with him, Ellis had no soul left. It might have been Cassis who'd brought Sienna into their fold, but Ellis was the one who accepted it. He'd been their leader, and he'd failed spectacularly.

But the realm itself? With its magic and lack of humans, with no need to hide who he was, that was home. "Very much so," Ellis answered honestly and, before Asher could follow up on the topic, walked out of the office.

A FEW HOURS LATER, Ellis opened the door to his room from the hallway and felt his entire body tense at the familiar smell. Although he couldn't see the male just yet, he knew Bryant was here.

Sure enough, as he closed the door behind him and stepped farther into the room, a large gray wolf who'd been dozing behind a bookshelf shook himself awake and stepped into view. The air shimmered about the way it always did here in the mortal world, and a few moments later, Bryant in all his glory was taking up Ellis's chair.

"Well, look at that uniform." The fae king's gaze raked over Ellis, a smirk twisting his strong features. His blond hair was brushed back from his high forehead, his blue eyes sharp as ever. "You look proper enough for a golden badge. I think that's what humans give out?"

Ellis's jaw tightened. He wasn't surprised that Bryant had managed to get his way past Victor's security to stage this little ambush, but he *was* surprised that his father had bothered with it. There was no reason to be stealthy—the king of Talon could walk through the front gates of the Academy any time he wished, probably to a full fucking reception. Which meant he had something specific—and covert—in mind.

"Father." Ellis bowed his head in proper deference and remained standing as Bryant sprawled his large body in Ellis's chair and continued regarding him for long moments.

"Well?" the king finally said. "Are you going to give me a report, or have you already forgotten what the hell I sent you here to do?"

Right. *Breaking the witch to bridle.* The notion had a rather different ring to it now than it had back in Bryant's study. Sticking his hands into his pockets, Ellis shrugged with swaggering nonchalance. If Bryant suspected that Ellis cared for Sam, he would exploit the weakness. Just as Sienna had exploited Reese's love of his wife.

"The witch is fully engaged in the Academy, as you commanded," Ellis said. "She is learning discipline—no small feat, as I've never met anyone who lacked it quite as much as she does."

"Look in the mirror next time you need to see what an undisciplined brat looks like," Bryant said. "Either way, there's a change of plans. One that will please you. You are being released from purgatory early. Return to Talon and take the witch with you."

Ellis schooled his face, his mind racing to pick apart his father's new orders. "Taking the witch through the gateway would be a violation of all the council's edicts. 'No nonfae shall ever enter Talon' and all that business. Isn't that why this whole charade of taking her to Talonswood Reform came about to begin with? So we could keep an eye on her here instead?"

"Yes, and had Asher not royally fucked everything up and handed the Academy to Victor on a silver platter, I'd have stayed the course." Bryant sighed as he rubbed his chin. "The count's presence changes the risk calculator too greatly. He is going to get his hooks into the witch somehow, I'm certain of it."

"You think Victor is going to beat me to securing the witch's obedience," Ellis said flatly.

"I don't think it, I'm damn certain of it." Bryant rose, moving the chair back into place. "I would like you to make it appear as if the witch ran away. Does she go into the town on a regular basis?"

Ellis considered lying, but the risk that Bryant already knew the answer was too great. "She does. Devinee is a bartender at Dusk. Next shift is this Saturday—so, three days."

"Bartender or snack?" Bryant shook his head. "Good enough. Have her take a detour and head to the gateway instead."

"You want me to kidnap her en route to Dusk and force her into the gateway?" Ellis clarified.

"I don't want you anywhere near her when she goes," Bryant snapped as if that much was obvious. "A rogue witch running away from Victor's cruelty. I can sell that." Bryant added the last to himself, plans already flashing though his dark-blue eyes.

It was a good cover story, Ellis had to admit. And Bryan would do an excellent job selling it to the council. Ellis snorted. "You want me to just give Devinee directions to the gateway and expect her to voluntarily prance off to Talon, a place she's never been?"

"That was—is—your damn job," Bryant barked, his face darkening. "Finish it. Say whatever you need to get it done. Lost puppy, ice cream, a key to unlock her magic—I don't care if you tell her she's the long-lost queen of the fae and needs to return to claim her throne, just get her there."

"Easy enough." Ellis's chest tightened, the effort it took to keep his fingers from clenching great enough that he did not dare take his hands out of his pockets. Nonetheless, something about his posture must have raised suspicion, because Bryant stilled suddenly, his piercing gaze narrowing on Ellis. "Is there something happening between you and the witch?"

Fuck.

Pushing away from the wall, Ellis sprawled lazily on his bed. "I wouldn't say no to a chance to stick my cock in the witch, but other than that, I've got no love for the damn thing."

"Get the *damn thing* to Talon, and you can stick your cock inside her anytime you wish." Without saying another word, a gray wolf took the place of the king of Talon and leapt gracefully out the window and into the night.

Waiting until he was sure Bryant was out of hearing range, Ellis shoved himself off the bed and reached for his phone. "Asher. We need Devinee confined to campus through the weekend. Something seemingly unexpected that comes up at the last moment is best. I'll fill you in in person."

31

Bryant

*B*ryant walked into the Talon gateway building, a large, modern glass-and-steel structure on a lush green hill overlooking downtown Talonswood. Of course, the building itself looked nothing like the actual centuries-old gateway to Talon housed deep underneath it. The security guards snapped to attention with such crispness that Bryant was certain the outside patrol had alerted them of his approach. Good. None of this lounging against the wall with hands in pockets that Ellis imagined he had a right to.

Bryant straightened his jacket lapels, setting course for his chief of security, Fryer. As his steps echoed over the marble floor, he considered his meeting with Ellis. Something about it hadn't felt right, and not just the insolence. In fact, the insolence bothered Bryant the least just now, because, while annoying, it was typical for the angry pup. If anything, Ellis hadn't been insolent enough. The boy had never been good at controlling his emotions, and his fury over being confined to a cadet's uniform in the human realm should have made the walls shudder.

The Ellis that Bryant knew would have all but taken a swing at him, not agreed to his orders with a minimum of negotiation. Then again, the last time Ellis had a run-in with a witch, he'd come crawling back on his belly. Maybe his time in Talonswood Reform had left him in a similar state of mind.

Either way, Fryer had a paranoid streak that would help them figure it out quickly enough.

"Well?" Bryant asked by way of welcome, motioning for his chief of security to remain behind the monitoring terminals. A short, thick-limbed man who shifted into a wolf the exact color of his wiry copper hair, Fryer was married to his work. He appeared to be in his zone now, and so Bryant let him stay that way—destroying people's productivity for the sake of vanity was a vampire tradition not a fae one. "Did you pick up anything?"

Fryer nodded, punching some keys on the computer. "The transmitter you placed picked up audio as soon you left the room. Here."

Bryant pulled up a chair and accepted the set of headphones. A moment later, Ellis's voice—distant but clear enough—filled his ears.

"Asher. We need Devinee confined to campus through the weekend. Something seemingly unexpected that comes up at the last moment is best. I'll fill you in in person."

Bryant's jaw tightened, and he met Fryer's unsurprised look. Fryer was suspicious of everyone and everything, and this time, his gloomy outlook had proved true. Not letting his simmering anger show on his face, Bryant put the headphones down, taking care with Fryer's equipment. As much as Bryant wanted to go right back to Talonswood and wring his wayward offspring's neck, discipline would have to wait. "It's worse than I thought. The pup is directly flouting my orders."

"What would you like me to do, Your Highness?" Fryer's eyes—one blue, one moss-green—were eerily riveted on him, making Bryant want to look away. A strange male, Fryer, but he got the job done.

Bryant considered. He was taking the witch to Talon, whether his bastard son helped him or not. The bloodsucker count had had too many weeks to sink his claws into her already.

Of course, Victor couldn't know Bryant had taken her by force—it could incite a second immortal world war—which meant he would need total plausible deniability.

"What's *Flood's* status?" he asked suddenly, an idea taking shape.

A corner of Fryer's mouth twitched in pleasure. *Flood* was Fryer's pet project, one that only someone as obsessed with conspiracy theories and paranoia as Fryer was would think up. In short, it was a group of shifter fae mercenaries who thought themselves employed by wealthy human creature hunters and had no idea that Fryer signed their paychecks.

The genius came in the backstories Fryer had created for them—backstories with enough layers to ensure *Flood* could never be traced back to Talon. The result was a group of freedom fighters at Bryant's beck and call. If the thing was done right, using them would leave Bryant untarnished— especially since Bryant himself would be there in harm's way.

On the flip side, this all meant that *Flood's* membership was made of glorified thugs too stupid to think through what they were doing.

Fryer had been itching for a chance to test *Flood* in a live mission for years now, and Bryant had thought the tool ludicrously blunt for just as long a time. Ultimately, however, a tool's value was based on how well it was suited for a particular job. And just now, blunt and stupid was a good thing.

"At ready simmer, sir. Thirty-hour window for full deployment."

Bryant nodded approvingly. That was better than expected. "And their backstory?"

"See for yourself, sir." Fryer punched something on his laptop, and one of the screens on the wall changed obediently from security footage to internet search results. News articles spanning decades populated the screen. Most of the stories in the mainstream human papers spoke about wolf attacks, though a dark web discussion thread made clear allusions to an unholy alliance between a rogue pack of shifter fae and a sect of human Hunters hell-bent on collecting shifter pelts.

"None of these events actually happened?" Bryant clarified.

Fryer made a vague motion with his hand. "The Hunter attacks happened for the most part. But I injected our people's involvement after the fact—completely without a trace."

"I see." Bryant tapped his finger on the table. "In that case, it's time to test out your freedom fighters, Fryer. Tell them… Tell them they get a bonus for body count, but the witch is to be brought out alive."

Fryer tried and failed to hide his pleasure. But for all his brainpower and conspiracy theories, the male never saw what was right in front of him—that Bryant couldn't care less whether he returned Fryer's toys in one piece.

In fact, Count Victor would be grateful when Bryant rushed in to warn him of an imminent attack against his academy. Bryant swallowed a chuckle. And who could say? Maybe this would even be a step in the right direction for diplomacy.

32

Sam

$\mathcal{I}$ examine the complicated combination lock, carefully tracing the new closing rune from another of Victor's precious pages. Around me, the deserted windowless chem lab is as cold and sterile as always, with its high metal stools and cold black countertops, each cut perfectly to accommodate a small sink for every workstation.

The lock in my hand finally snaps into place on my fiftieth time drawing the rune, and I smell a hint of burned magnesium touch the air, as if I just lit a sparkler. The thought of my magic having a smell is a bit disconcerting, but at least it's better than the scents of bleach and Lysol that the vamps use to wash down the lab daily.

Turning the now-engaged lock over in my hands, I sigh in pleasant relief at my success, though I have a bit of a headache from concentrating. Admittedly, entering the lock's code would have been a far faster way of closing the damn thing, but Victor insists doing this will help hone my precision.

To his credit, I am seeing progress. A week ago, I could barely close a crude padlock.

Whatever else can be said about Victor, the male has kept his word about giving me the space and tools to start developing my skills.

A familiar ping of guilt crunches my belly over keeping Ellis and Reese in the dark, but I can't have another argument over using my magic with the males right now. If Reese got his way, I wouldn't be touching magic for a few centuries—which might work if I was fucking immortal. I stretch my back. I mean I'm not *totally* secret squirrel. Mika knows. And Cassis. Once the vamp comes through with a text to replace Victor's, I'll at least have someone on my side when I ease the other males into my routine.

Plus, if I'm going to be practicing magic on school grounds, I shouldn't be feeling guilty about the headmaster himself signing off on the project. Right?

Putting the lock back in the cabinet where I keep my supplies, I draw a basic closing rune on it and smile as the little latch clicks into place. The clock on the wall reads 6:30 p.m., though it feels later. I should get a good night's sleep before tomorrow, when my shift at Dusk keeps me up half the night.

Turning off the lights, I head into the empty hallway, my phone vibrating in my pocket as soon as I enter the hallway. The chem lab has zero reception, and at least five missed calls from Ellis are flashing on the screen. "You better work outside," I tell the phone, which may have condescended to show a missed call screen, but has no intention of actually connecting to a network in here.

"Talking to inanimate objects, are we?"

I jump at the sound, my heart racing as I realize I'm not—as I'd thought—alone in an empty hallway.

Their steps light, Wayne the Wolverine and a pair of his

cronies prowl toward me, a fourth—in wolf form—bringing up the rear. Wolves aren't the only animal that fae shift into, but it seems the most common around here, possibly something to do with the royal line that Ellis and Asher come from.

"A witch walks into a chemistry lab," Wayne says to Bea, the gorgeous blonde at his side. "Does that sound like an opening to a joke from a horror movie?"

"Bubble, bubble, toil and trouble." Bea grins, showing sharp canines. "Looks like somebody desperately needed a cauldron."

Fuck.

I look over my shoulder, and, sure enough, two more cadets are there. Wayne's entire little pack. The same one which Asher whipped over the initial run-in with me and the vamps.

The same one from which Victor let me walk away scot-free.

Gripping my phone, I punch in Ellis's number, cursing as the reception flickers out completely.

Bea clicks her tongue. With the next motion, she sprints forward, snatching the phone from my hands. "See, witch, we believe in fairness," she says, her British accent as clean and perfect as the rest of her. "Do you believe in that? You are from America, aren't you? Something about justice for all?"

"Your civics knowledge is unparalleled." My heart pounds, my hands curling into fists, though I'm not stupid enough to think I can fight them off. Plan B, then. Walk with a purpose, worry about the phone later.

I start toward the exit.

Wayne takes a step in front of me, cutting off my path, his yellow-green eyes lit with a terrifying amusement in the fluorescent hallway light. "See, that part about *justice*," he says.

"It seems there isn't very much of that when it comes to you, Sam-bitch. We thought that might bother you. Make you feel left out, you know?"

Before I can move, someone grabs me from behind, a sweaty hand clamping over my mouth. My heart pounds, my heels scraping against the floor as the lot drag me back toward the lab.

"Get her key," Wayne orders, making my stomach sink further.

Whoever's holding me from behind wrenches my arms back as Bea pats me down—then plunges her hand into my jeans' back pocket. With my legs still free, I try to stomp down on the foot of whoever is holding me, but Wayne grabs my hair and pulls my head back at an angle.

"Listen to me, Sam-witch," he says, his gaze full of unfiltered menace, a noxious scent of bloody meat drifting into my face. His dark hair and sideburns are slicked with sweat. "Either quietly take your fair share of the punishment and we'll call things even, or make enough of a kind of fuss that will get Asher's attention. None of us are eager for another trip to his office, so if you create that problem, we'll pay it back tenfold. So you understand me?"

I draw a quick breath. Of course I understand him. I learned about snitches and stitches by age six. But not snitching and not fighting are two fucking different things.

The door to the chem lab clicks open behind me, and as the asshole twists me around, I manage to get my arm free. Fingers curled into a fist, I swing right at Bea's perfect nose. And *shit*, it seems Ellis and Reese knew what they were teaching, because the feel of crunching cartilage beneath my knuckles is a surprise to her and me both.

"Bitch!" Bea hollers, blood streaming down her face. She pulls back her fist, but Wayne grabs her wrist.

"Stand down and stay to the plan," he orders her, a growl rumbling through his wide chest as I'm forced into the chem lab and tripped flat onto the floor. "What do we have here?"

I have a moment to wonder what *here* refers to, before Wayne and Bea appear in my line of vision again, each holding a jug of bleach cleaner the chem lab keeps next to the mops. Opening the lids, the pair pours the bleach all over me, the caustic stench making me cough as I struggle against their hold.

"You really should be careful with this stuff," Wayne says, his image blurry behind my watering eyes. "Don't want to get bleach spilled all over yourself."

I gasp, choking for air even as the asshole lets me go. As I crawl to my hands and knees, cough after cough tearing through my chest, I hear the bastards lock the door behind them as they leave.

33

Ellis

*E*llis cursed, rereading Asher's text. Apparently, Bryant had given up his stealth-mode visits and was now meeting openly with Victor.

It made no sense. As far as the king was concerned, all was going according to plan, with Sam being groomed to prance off to the Talon gateway the following day, just as he'd asked. The king should have been keeping himself as distant as possible from the Academy, not walking through the front gates.

What does he want? Ellis tapped into his phone.

A flip-off emoji flashed in reply. Well, it was a stupid question—if Asher knew why their father was here, he'd have told him.

Ellis reached for the keys again. ***You tell anyone about confining Devinee to campus?***

Worried about tipping the hand too early and needing to ensure Sam had a genuine reaction to the news, they'd decided to let Asher make a last-minute disciplinary decree first and explain the reason right after. But if Asher had started socializing the issue...

No.

Right. Feeling his chest tighten uncomfortably, Ellis dialed Sam's number, growling as the phone went to voice mail. Either the girl had it turned off like a good little cadet should, or she was in one of the too-many dead-reception zones. Despite knowing the result, Ellis tapped Sam's number again and again as he walked over to her room, his heart speeding. Whatever reason Bryant had to be back on campus, and this time overtly, Ellis didn't like it.

"Devinee?" Ellis opened the door to Sam's room without bothering to knock. The place was neat as usual, Sam's sweet scent hanging enticingly in the air.

"Not here." Sitting at her laptop, Mika barely glanced up at Ellis's intrusion, her attention firmly on her computer screen. "That's strange. Did you just leave your room door open?"

Ellis ignored the strange question and held out his screen of missed calls toward Mika. "Devinee isn't answering her phone. Do you know where she is?"

Mika's gaze flicked over Ellis's screen. "You called her five times? That's called stalking. If she wants to answer you, she will." Mika's computer beeped, drawing the demi's attention. "Did you leave your door open, Ellis?"

Ellis rubbed his hand over his face, reminding himself that shaking Mika until her neck snapped would be unlikely to help his cause. Especially since Mika had a point—after weeks of him avoiding Sam, the witch did not owe Ellis an explanation of her every step.

"Earth to Ellis," said Mika. "Door?"

Ellis turned to walk out before he did something he regretted.

"An odd signal just appeared on the network," Mika said behind him, stopping him in his tracks. "I've seen it pop up briefly over the past two days, but I'm picking it up steadily now. I imagine there's a line-of-sight issue. Which means if your door is open, then it's coming from your room."

Ellis's heart stuttered, blood draining from his face. "There's something transmitting from my room?"

Mike threw up her hands. "I know, I just said as much, for fuck's sake. Can you turn it off or keep your door closed? It's annoying."

Ellis cursed, his mind racing. Bryant had bugged his room, had heard everything Ellis said. Which meant he knew Ellis had no intention of delivering Sam to him tomorrow. And now the king was here, doing fuck knows what with Victor. Grabbing a pen and piece of paper from Mika's desk, Ellis scribbled, *Don't say anything aloud.*

Mika's eyes widened, her scent spiking with fear. Good. Ellis didn't have time to cajole.

Devinee is in danger, he wrote quickly. *Where is she?*

Grabbing the pen from Ellis's hand, Mika wrote two words. *Chem lab.*

Not bothering to ask what in the bloody hell the witch was doing there, Ellis pulled out his phone to text Asher the update —only to find the phone already vibrating.

Asher: ***Found out why Bryant came. He has intel— attack on Academy by rogue fae imminent. Just warned Victor. I'm sounding lockdown.***

Ten seconds later, just as Ellis dashed to his room for his sword and started slinging the scabbard over his back, an ear-piercing alarm wailed through Talonswood Reform.

34

Sam

*a*n ear-piercing lockdown alarm blares through the loudspeakers as I yank on the locked chem lab door over and over. My head swims, my throat closing from the bleach's caustic fumes. A drip from my hair touches my eye, and I scream at the burn, but the demifae on the other side of the door do nothing.

My heart races, my mind unable to think. I'm locked in. I can't breathe. I can't leave. I can't can't can't.

"Let me out!" I scream to Wayne and the others as I throw my body against the door, the heavy wood rattling against the hinges but failing to give. "Let me—cahhh…" I choke on the words, unable to take in the breath to scream again.

"Lockdown has been initiated. Shelter in place or get to fortified location," a computerized voice announces over the intercom. *"This is not a drill. I repeat, this is not a drill. A lockdown had been…"*

I try to hold my breath, afraid of pulling any more poisonous fumes into my lungs. My pulse pounds so quickly that it makes me dizzy, the realization that Wayne and his pack must have left with the alarm's sounding sending a new wave of terror through me.

I slide down to the floor, forcing my mind to work. To think. To concentrate. Whatever is happening out there, it can be no worse than the death waiting for me here. And if there's one thing training with the damn males has taught me, it's that being miserable—or halfway dead—is no excuse to stop thinking.

Think, Sam, I command myself. *Want to live? Then think. You are locked in. You need to get out. Open the damn door.*

Right. Dipping the tip of my finger into the liquid bleach soaking my clothes, I draw the opening rune Ellis once showed me, the wet streaks crude on the wooden door.

Nothing happens. Not on my first attempt. Or the second. Or the tenth. I'm no longer feeling anything as I try again and again, all my focus and concentration zeroing on nothing but the painful details. On my thirteenth try, I feel it, the buzzing of bees inside my blood, the energy that tells me my magic is working.

Then… *Click.*

The sound of the lock opening makes me whimper with relief. Gasping, I grab for the door handle. My hand closes around it just as a drop of liquid from the top part of the rune snakes down the drawing. My heart stops as a I see a line now cutting through the whole damn picture, my magic still connected to the spell.

Fucking gravity is all I have time to think before launching myself away from the door just before the whole thing explodes. And not just the door, which flies off its hinges. Beakers, containers, the clock—everything in the room shatters with a spectacular fountain of shards. To top it off, as

I take cover beneath one of the metal tables, a long crack takes hold in the wall facing the green.

If anyone didn't know where I was before, they sure do now.

"Samantha!" Reese punches his fist through the crumpling wall, his hand bloody as he moves away the debris. "Samantha!"

"Here," I try to shout, though the sound comes out in choking fits.

The Reese who shoves his way into the chem lab is nothing like the aloof instructor I've come to expect. With crisp movements, he checks the corners and blind spots of the room, a trained and honed military machine. Even after his gaze marks my location, he finishes scanning the room before grabbing the front of my shirt and dragging me out from under the table.

"Bleach?" he asks with a preternatural calm, his nostrils flaring delicately as he takes in my state.

I manage to nod.

Before I can say a word, Reese is ripping off all my clothes and dragging me naked to the back of the room. Confusion rushes through my muddled brain, my hands digging into Reese's powerful forearm. I don't know what the male thinks he's doing, but I know I need out of this room, not deeper into it.

"Shower," Reese says in that too-calm voice of his, as if the word is code for something that makes sense. Though a moment later, it actually does, as the vamp pulls some kind of rope hanging off the ceiling and gallons of freezing water dump themselves onto my head. Who the hell knew there was a shower in the damn lab all along?

"A pack of rogue fae are attacking the Academy," Reese says, pulling off his black T-shirt to give to me, his unsheathed sword held at the ready. With splashes of water on his smooth, pale skin, he seems to glisten under the harsh lab lights. "This room now has too many entrance points to defend. We need to move to a better position."

"Humans hunters?" I pant now that I can breathe again, though my hands shake as I pull on the male's shirt. Seems Asher and the nonstop drills he held before Victor showed up had it right.

"Rogue shifter fae," Reese says, glancing over his shoulder at me. "Why are you here with bleach all over you?"

"Practicing magic." I adjust the hem of his shirt, which hangs just to my thighs, and my attention follows Reese's gaze to where the crack in the wall is spreading with silent determination. Given that the chem lab is about to be missing a wall, there seems little point in lying now.

"In the chemistry lab?"

"That's where Victor told me to do it."

Reese's body stills, his cool blue eyes swinging toward me. "Victor. You've been practicing magic in secret with Victor." The vamp holds his hand up, forestalling my answer as he peers out through the opening to the green. Despite his calm tone and crisp movements, the male's jaw clenches hard enough that I can see a muscle ticking in his chiseled chin. "The attackers have breached the green, but we have a clear path to the gymnasium now."

I nod, though Reese can't see me, my pulse picking up speed. The gym and barracks are our shelter locations, the ones I've gone to many times in drills. Except now it's for real.

As if scenting the healthy dose of anxiety that just spilled into my blood, Reese spares a glance toward me. "I need to you to stay right beside me, Samantha. Eyes on me. Your attention on me. Nowhere else." Despite the shouting I can already hear coming from the other side of the wall, Reese's voice stays even and confident, his strong fingers reaching out to touch my chin. "Do that, and I promise I'll get you to the gym safely. Do you understand?"

"Can we stay here?" As if hearing my question, the building creaks ominously, a piece of the ceiling crashing down onto a nearby table. "Never mind. Let's go."

Reese nods once. "Let's move," he orders sharply, then leads the pair of us onto a green that looks nothing like the one I remember.

35

Sam

The blazing siren continues to sound as students rush over the grass toward garrison points, the rumbling chaos resembling nothing of Asher's once-constant drills. Wind whistles through the air, billowing my shirt, my bare feet slipping against cold grass. The setting sun casts the whole world in brilliant pink-and-orange light—the lamps will come on soon, but the darkness will still give full fae an advantage over demis.

I try to keep my eyes on Reese as instructed, but manage only two heartbeats before the first ear-piercing scream snares my attention.

Turning my head, I see a pack of two dozen wolves rushing onto the green through the front gates, which have been smashed down, their graceful gray bodies leaping through the air. As one wolf after another streams into the open, the air around the predators shimmers, leaving grim fatigues-clad warriors in the animals' place. The first three to shift swing their swords without bothering to look, and the next scream has a familiar voice.

Christian, Victor's pet vamp, goes down with a blade sticking out of his eye. A moment later, Wayne and his fledgling pack are cut down as they try to outrun the immortals. My breath catches, my feet tripping on the grass.

This isn't battle, I realize as my knees bang against the ground. It's a mindless killing spree.

A strong hand closes on my upper arm, Reese's steady voice and tangy scent cutting though my haze. "On your feet, Samantha," the vamp says into my ear as if nothing at all is happening around us. "You are with me. It's a hundred-yard sprint now. Nice and easy."

I swallow and scramble back to my feet—only to stop dead as a familiar form jumps clear out of the second-story window of the cadets' barracks, pale blond hair streaming behind him. Landing in a perfect crouch, Ellis moves with predator's grace, his sword an extension of his body. He cuts two thugs' throats before I can draw one breath. Again. Again. Again.

Screams and howls batter my eardrums.

I can feel shock sinking into my blood, my fingertips, my brain. I've never seen so many immortals in one place. I've never seen so much blood.

From the edges of the green, a host of Academy guards and instructors are coming to join the fight, others breaking out to herd the last of the cadets to the garrison points. But they don't matter to me. Not when all I see is Ellis in the middle of a storm, dancing with his sword. Blood, at least some of it his, soaks his shirt. His face is calm and deadly. As is Asher's as he joins the fight at his brother's left side.

"Move," Reese orders, yanking on my arm. "They're buying us time, Sam. Let's go."

"That's her!" A dark-bearded male across the green points

his sword right at me, the long blade catching blood-orange sunset light like a streak of fire. "That's her! Get the witch!"

My blood chills to ice. Me. This is happening because of me.

Reese curses, yanking me so hard that I nearly lose my footing as he starts us back into a sprint. But we aren't the only ones running.

As if turned with the tide, a pack of five attackers separates from the main melee and head directly for us at an angle, half of them turning into wolves midstride to gain speed.

The hundred yards between us and the garrison point at the gymnasium are suddenly miles long, no matter how hard my legs pump against the ground. We're halfway to safety when the pack intercepts us. Reese spins between me and a shifting fae, taking the tip of a sword in his shoulder. I scream, but Reese only grunts and strikes back immediately, his movements too fast for me to follow—until I hear the crunch of bone as Reese cleanly breaks the first attacker's neck.

"Run, Samantha," he orders, his voice steel, his body sinking into a defensive crouch to meet the coming rogue. Reese doesn't sound scared at all, but I know well enough what happens when bare hands fight steel. Know that if I run, this will be the last time I ever see him.

A dam inside me bursts open, letting in the rage and fear and enough fucking determination to down the whole damn world. It's me the jackasses are here for, and they will not spill my males' blood. *My males.* Rage fills me, bees buzzing and crackling inside my blood.

I spread my bare feet against the grass, feeling the cold grounding earth beneath me as the world around me seems too slow, each movement and sound and smell its own distinct thread.

The copper of blood mixing with the sweet scent of fresh-cut grass.

The cold wind cutting across my damp skin, the sensation simultaneously stinging and energizing.

Threads of saliva whipping back from a gray wolf's lip as it hurtles through the air.

My males. Ellis's powerful legs kicking a foe so hard that the male goes airborne before falling. Asher taking a slash across his biceps to protect his brother's back. Reese twisting an attacker's arm while another readies to sink his sword into the back of Reese's neck.

"Stop," I yell, and I feel my command crackle through the thick, thick air. The buzzing in my blood intensifies, growing louder and louder until I'm certain the whole green must hear it. Must feel how overfull, how saturated the whole damn world has suddenly become, the pressure building and building until—

Until it suddenly gives with a clap of thunder and lightning, the energy surging from both the unnaturally gathering clouds and *me*.

The witch they came here to capture.

Sinking an invisible hand into my thick, palpable magic, I launch it right at the male holding his sword at Reese's neck. It feels like launching a grenade, except instead of exploding, the little bubble of magic becomes a target for a live jolt of electricity crackling down from the sky.

The male has no chance to scream before he falls, and I have no time to watch his demise. Focusing my power, I bring it down onto the green in a rhythmic *crack crack crack* of lightning, throwing my targets where I want them, spinning to launch the next before even waiting to check my aim. I beat out a circle all around the battleground, taking out those warriors who still dare to stand against us.

Crack. Crack. Crack.

Rain streams from the sky, each bolt of lightning eliminating the night's growing darkness. The power vibrates through me like music along the strings of Cassis's piano. Ready to be played. To be turned into a beautiful melody or a deadly crescendo of notes. When my next crack of power reflects off a downed sword, I snatch the steel from the ground and hold it above my head, attracting a bolt of lightning that flows through me with gentle warmth, grounding in the earth below my feet.

"Get. Out!" I yell over the momentary silence, my control over my magic slipping at last with a final great *crack* hitting the crumpling chem lab.

The rogue wolves need no further invitation to flee.

3 6

Sam

Of all things I expect to happen next, the sound of
applause is far down the list. Yet, as I stand there,
naked beneath Reese's oversized shirt, the sound of exactly
one person clapping rings through the singed air.

Dressed impeccably as always, in a dark suit and bloodred
tie, Victor walks toward me with a small smile in his black eyes.
King Bryant walks beside him, the wet grass squelching under
his expensive loafers, his face unreadable. The quietness
around the green changes, even the whimpers of the wounded
becoming subdued in the background as I raise my chin and
meet the two males' penetrating gazes.

My heart pounds against my chest as they stop before me,
and I tighten my hand around the hot hilt of my new sword.
Its smooth leather grip makes me feel less vulnerable—not that
I'd have any idea what to do with the thing.

Though the rain is continuing to pour, the high of energy
still buzzes inside me.

"Well, it is a day of most unexpected events, isn't it?" Victor says with a cold smile, directing the words more to Bryant than to me.

Slightly shorter than Victor, the tanklike Bryant—who I last saw wearing a public defender's disguise—tips his head in acknowledgment. When his blue eyes meet mine, however, the hate and fury inside them is enough to make my blood chill.

"I do thank you for bringing us forewarning of the attack, Bryant," Victor continues, giving the fae king a short bow. "Your timeliness doubtless saved many lives."

"It was the least I could do." Bryant returns the bow, the tension between the men as palpable as my magic. "No leader likes to learn that rogue packs fester in his realm, but I thought mitigating the potential damage was the immediate priority. But it seems you had everything well in hand, Victor." The king turns to me, his thin lips hardening almost imperceptibly. "I am a bit surprised, though, that you permit the witch quite such free rein on her magic. Are you certain it is safe for all cadets?"

I feel movement behind me, Reese's minty ocean tang letting me know that he's near, his quiet support calming my nerves. A few paces away, Ellis is inching his way toward me as well, though the male is careful to look anywhere but my face.

"She surprised us all." Victor opens his palms, his hawk-eyed gaze clipping me for a moment. "Now that we know the magnitude of Samantha's power, however, I'm certain we will be in a good position to help her harness it. The Academy *is* the place for just that, after all. Will you be making the report to the council about the attack, or should I take care of the paperwork for both of us?"

"I would never burden you with my paperwork, Count Victor." Despite his generous tone, Bryant's jaw is so tight that a vein pulses visibly along his temple. "Allow me to ease your job in one small way, though—I will take my delinquent pup home where he belongs. Ellis. Get your things."

My throat tightens, the elation lingering from the battle morphing to a heart-pounding ache.

Bryant's eyes narrow on me. "Is something the matter, Samantha?" he asks.

I don't know what to say. Don't even know what Ellis wants, given the male's frozen silence, his opaque golden eyes.

Bryant snaps his fingers, pointing to a spot right in front of him. "Ellis."

My stomach sinks as Ellis obeys, the beautiful, battle-torn male walking obediently toward the king. Three steps away. Two. With the final strong stride, Ellis steps…right beside me and turns crisply on his heels.

"No." The single word crashes between the king and him with a finality that I know is deeper than I fully understand.

Bryant's eyes widen, surprise and fury flashing in their blue depths. "That wasn't a suggestion, Ellis."

"And my answer was not a debate," Ellis replies.

Behind me, Reese draws a rare breath. I know that provoking Bryant in the middle of the green was unlikely a wise move on Ellis's part, but the male's words flood me with relief anyway.

Victor clears his throat, his hand covering his mouth.

"Let me phrase it another way," Bryant says, his low, menacing voice promising pain to come. "You return to Talon with me now, or you will never be allowed to step foot there again."

Ellis stiffens beside me, and I know Bryant has hit so deep that I would not blame Ellis for leaving. Not with what the asshole king is threatening. Talon is Ellis's home. The key to the male's magic. The missing piece that always hangs at the corner of his mood, weighting him down with its absence.

Never is a very long time for an immortal. Much longer than a witch's tiny life span.

"Well?" Bryant presses. "Have you made your decision?"

"Aye. I have." Taking hold of my shoulders, Ellis turns me toward him and seals his mouth over mine with a possessive heat that chases the entire rest of the world away.

"So, are you still upset over me using magic?" I ask Reese as he and Ellis walk me back to my room.

Just moments ago, Victor escorted a red-with-fury Bryant off the green—and presumably back to his armored car and out of our lives. Asher immediately set to work restoring order at the Academy, cleaning up the battleground, organizing the wounded, and making arrangements for the ten cadets who died.

"You really don't want to know what I think," Reese murmurs, the low warning in his voice making my sex grow damp and warm, especially when his hand snakes casually down my spine to my ass. Fuck. The fact that I'm half-naked and they are not is utterly unfair.

Ellis leads the way into the cadets' barracks, the three of us climbing the steps together. I sniff audibly. "Well, I think you both need a shower."

Ellis turns back to give me a predatory look over his shoulder. "Watch yourself, witch. You have no idea what battle fever does to a wolf."

I swallow, my breath quickening. Fuck everything. I just want to get to my room, and then we can discuss exactly whose battle fever is—

"Stop it! No! Nooooo!" Mika's wail seeps out from under

our door into the hallway, sending the three of us into an all-out sprint.

Reaching the door first, Ellis doesn't bother knocking before throwing his shoulder against it, the door giving beneath his force. A moment later, his curses join my roommate's, and Reese grabs the back of my neck with a growl to keep my ass behind him.

"Status?" Reese asks, blocking my final step to the door with his arm.

"See for your bloody self," Ellis calls out.

Shoving Reese aside, I rush into my room—and stop dead.

Down feathers, which once lived inside my two pillows, are now covering the entire space, the rest of the bed in similar cotton bits. My clothes, what's left of them, have likewise been pulled from the dresser and shredded.

All courtesy of a little green…lizard monster thing that is now happily reducing my wooden chair to ash.

"Where did that come from?" I demand.

Mike throws up her hands. "The window." She points to the broken glass. "I don't know where it was before that. Or why it's here now."

"It…it hatched," Ellis says quietly. "And, I wager, hitched a ride here with my father without the bastard knowing."

I spin on him. "You know what this thing is?"

"Of course," Ellis says, meeting my gaze. "And so do you."

I watch, my heart pounding for some reason I can't explain.

The dragon—because that's what it is—waddles around unsteadily, seeming unnerved by the larger audience.

But then it's dark little eyes find mine.

Sam! Sam! Sam! a familiar voice purrs inside my soul. The same voice I once heard from a ruby-red egg.

"Fuck," I mutter, staring right back at the little creature.

Noting my attention, the dragon starts flapping his wings and making small cooing sounds. And then it burps a burst of flame that destroys my favorite boots.

THE ADVENTURE CONTINUES in LAST CHANCE WITCH, Immortals of Talonswood Book 3. If you are reading an ebook version of this book, please continue for a FREE preview of Alex Lidell's best-selling reverse harem fantasy romance, POWER OF FIVE.

SCOUT

TRACING SHADOWS (Audiobook available)

UNRAVELING DARKNESS (Audiobook available)

TILDOR

THE CADET OF TILDOR

SIGN UP FOR NEW RELEASE NOTIFICATIONS at https://
links.alexlidell.com/News

ABOUT THE AUTHOR

Alex Lidell is an Amazon KU All Star Top 50 Author Awards winner (July, 2018). Her debut novel, THE CADET OF TILDOR (Penguin, 2013) was an Amazon Breakout Novel Awards finalist. Her Reverse Harem romances, POWER OF FIVE and MISTAKE OF MAGIC, both received Amazon KU Top 100 awards for individual titles.

Alex is an avid horseback rider, a (bad) hockey player, and an ice-cream addict. Born in Russia, Alex learned English in elementary school, where a thoughtful librarian placed a copy of Tamora Pierce's ALANNA in Alex's hands. In addition to becoming the first English book Alex read for fun, ALANNA started Alex's life long love for fantasy books. Alex lives in Washington, DC.

Join Alex's newsletter for news, special offers and sneak peeks: https://links.alexlidell.com/News

Find out more on Alex's website: www.alexlidell.com

SIGN UP FOR NEWS AND RELEASE NOTIFICATIONS

Connect with Alex!
www.alexlidell.com
alex@alexlidell.com

www.ingramcontent.com/pod-product-compliance
Lightning Source LLC
Chambersburg PA
CBHW050509190726
48284CB00003B/738